DIE, MY LOVE

CHARCO  PRESS

First published by Charco Press 2017

Charco Press Ltd., Office 59, 44-46 Morningside Road, Edinburgh EH10 4BF

This book was originally published in Spanish under the title
Matate, amor in 2012 by Lengua de Trapo (Spain), republished in 2017 by
Mardulce (Argentina).

Work published with funding from the 'Sur' Translation Support Program of
the Ministry of Foreign Affairs and Worship of Argentina / Obra editada en
el marco del Programa 'Sur' de Apoyo a las Traducciones del Ministerio de
Relaciones Exteriores y Culto de la República Argentina.

ISBN: 978 1 9997227 8 4
e-book: 978 1 9997227 9 1

www.charcopress.com

Edited by Annie McDermott
Cover design by Pablo Font
Typeset by Laura Jones

6   8   10   9   7   5

Ariana Harwicz

DIE, MY LOVE

Translated by
Sarah Moses & Carolina Orloff

CHARCO PRESS

I lay back in the grass among fallen trees and the sun on my palm felt like a knife I could use to bleed myself dry with one swift cut to the jugular. Behind me, against the backdrop of a house somewhere between dilapidated and homely, I could hear the voices of my son and my husband. Both of them naked. Both of them splashing around in the blue paddling pool, the water thirty-five degrees. It was the Sunday before a bank holiday. I was a few steps away, hidden in the underbrush. Spying on them. How could a weak, perverse woman like me, someone who dreams of a knife in her hand, be the mother and wife of those two individuals? What was I going to do? I burrowed deeper into the ground, hiding my body. I wasn't going to kill them. I dropped the knife and went to hang out the washing like nothing had happened. I carefully pegged the socks to the line, my baby's and my man's. Their underwear and shirts. I looked at myself and saw an ignorant country bumpkin hanging out the laundry and drying her hands on her skirt before returning to the kitchen. They had no idea. Hanging out the clothes had been a success. I lay back down among the tree trunks. They're already chopping wood for the cold season. People here prepare for winter like animals. Nothing distinguishes us from them. Take me, an educated woman, a university graduate – I'm more of an animal than those half-dead foxes, their faces stained red, sticks propping their mouths wide open. My neighbour Frank a few miles away, the oldest of seven siblings, fired a shotgun into his own arse last Christmas. What a nice surprise it must have been for his pack of kids. But the guy was just following tradition. Suicide by shotgun for his great-great-grandfather, great-grandfather, grandfather and father. At the very least, you could say it was his turn. And me? A normal woman from a normal family, but an eccentric, a deviant, the mother of one child and with another, though who knows at this point, on its way. I slowly slide a hand into my knickers. And to think I'm the person in charge of my son's education. My husband calls me over for a beer under the pergola, asks, Blonde or dark? The baby appears to have shat himself and I've got to go and buy his cake. I bet other mothers would bake one themselves. Six months, apparently it's not the same as five or seven. Whenever I look at him I think of my husband behind me, about to ejaculate on my back, but instead turning me over suddenly and coming inside me. If this hadn't happened, if I'd closed my legs, if I'd grabbed his dick, I wouldn't have to go to the bakery for cream cake or chocolate cake and candles, half a year already. The moment other women give birth they usually say, I can't imagine my life without him now, it's as though he's always been here. Pfff. I'm coming, baby! I want to scream, but I sink deeper into the cracked earth. I want to snarl, to howl, but instead I let the mosquitoes bite me, let them savour my sweetened skin. The sun deflects the silvery reflection of the knife back to me and I'm blinded. The sky is red, violet, trembling. I hear them looking for me, the filthy baby and the naked husband. Ma-ma, da-da, poo-poo. My baby's the one who does the talking, all night long. Co-co-na-na-ba-ba. There they are. I leave the knife in the scorched pasture, hoping that when I find it next it'll look like a scalpel, a feather, a pin. I get up, hot and bothered by the tingling between my legs. Blonde or dark? Whatever you're having, my love. We're one of those couples who mechanise the word 'love', who use it even when they despise each other. I never want to see you again, my love. I'm coming, I say, and I'm a fraud of a country woman with a red polka-dot skirt and split ends. I'll have a blonde beer, I say in my foreign accent. I'm a woman who's let herself go, has a mouth full of cavities and no longer reads. Read, you idiot, I tell myself, read one full sentence from start to finish. Here we are, all three of us together for a family portrait. We toast the happiness of our baby and drink the beers, my son in his high chair chewing on a leaf. I put a finger in his mouth and he shrieks, biting me with his gums. My husband wants to plant a tree for the baby's long life and I don't know what to say, I just smile like a fool. Does he have any idea? So many healthy and beautiful women in the area, and he ended up falling for me. A nutcase. A foreigner. Someone beyond repair. Muggy out today, isn't it? Seems it'll last a while, he says. I take long swigs from the bottle, breathing through my nose and wishing, quite simply, that I were dead.

I'm in my son's room, lit by a faint blue light. I watch my nipple satisfying him with every slurp. My husband – I've got used to calling him that by now – is smoking outside. I hear the puffs at regular intervals, fffff, fffff. The baby chokes on my milk and I lean him against my chest to burp him, ridding him of the air that gets trapped in his stomach, air from my milk, air from my chest, air from my insides. After he burps he becomes a dead weight. His arms hang by his sides, his eyelids thicken, his breath grows sluggish. I lay him down, wrapped up in my scarf, and while I swaddle him: Isadora Duncan. Who gets which life. What body do you end up in. I can no longer hear the smoke slipping between my husband's teeth. I throw out the heavy nappy and walk towards the patio doors. I always toy with the idea of going right through the glass and cutting every inch of my body, always aiming to pass through my own shadow. But just before I hit it, I stop myself and slide it open. Outside, my husband is pissing a stream the colour of the *mate* he was drinking earlier. I can see the hot, greenish-yellow drops cascading down the garage's corrugated metal. He turns and smiles at me with his hands on his limp, dripping member. Want to go and look at the stars? I've never been able to make him understand that I'm not interested in stars. That I'm not interested in what's in the sky. That I don't care about the telescope he's now struggling to carry to the bottom of the garden, where it slopes down into the woods. I don't want to count the stars, look at their shapes, see which is the brightest, learn why they're called Orion's Belt or the String of Pearls or the Big Dipper. He busies himself setting up his precious three-legged device. My husband's an enthusiastic kind of guy. Do you see the String of Pearls? Yes, dear. Look at those bright twinkling specks, don't you just want to eat them with your eyes? They're so tiny, and to think they're actually huge masses. No, I thought, I don't like illusions. Not optical illusions or auditory illusions, not sensory, olfactory or cerebral illusions. I don't like black objects in the sky. They make me feel alive, he says. Look at that constellation and try to jump from one star to the next as though you were crossing a rickety wooden bridge… And look at that face, it's like a skeleton! His elation hurts me. He hugs me, puts his arms around my shoulders. It's been months since we've hugged. We don't hold hands either, we're always pushing the buggy or carrying the baby instead. Do you see the Great Bear and the Little Bear? Yep, I say, and hug him, but my eyes linger in the starless space, in the absence of light. We face the threat of the dark sky above us, every night… A meteor! he shouted, letting go of me in his excitement. I missed it. You have to pay attention, you can only see them when they're close to the sun, and only for a split second. Didn't you see its trail? he asked, annoyed. Then he lit a cigarette and said, It's about getting your bearings in the sky. Look at that group of stars and follow an imaginary line, okay? It's no more difficult than reading a road map and following the dotted line so you don't end up in the sea. I thought the child might be crying, but I hear him crying every night and when I go to him I find absolute silence, as though a few seconds of his cries had been recorded and were playing back of their own accord. But sometimes I don't hear anything. I'm sitting on the sofa, a few feet from his room, watching a programme about wife-swapping or super-nannies, or painting my nails, when my dear husband appears, his underwear hanging low, and says: Why won't he stop crying? What does he want? You're his mother, you should know. But I don't know, I say, I haven't the faintest idea… Don't you find the moon relaxing? Go on up to the lens, take a look at the moon right now because it won't be the same tomorrow. Those grey craters, they make me want to eat it, smoke it even! I did look at the moon, but all I could think about was the sound of the baby crying, my body secreting, impatient for him to stop. The advice I was given by that young social worker who came to our house when my mother-in-law called, alarmed: 'If your child cries so much that you feel like you can't go on and you're about to lose control, get out of there. Leave the child with someone else and find a place where you can regain composure and calm. If you're alone and there's no one to leave him with, go somewhere else anyway. Leave the child in a safe place and take a few steps back.' If only there were *santiguadoras* living in these parts, those village women who for a flat fee will pray away your guy's indigestion and your toddler's tantrums, simple as that. I'd have liked to be aboard the Apollo, are you listening? Or any mission to outer space… Are you even paying attention? On the Apollo, watching the earth grow distant… Shhh! Is he crying? What do you mean, is he crying? I'm talking to you about the moon! The moon is just like you lot, come to think of it, he says. You all have your dark side. But I'm thinking about pacing up and down with the baby in my arms, hour after hour of tedious choreography, from the exhaustion to screaming, screaming to exhaustion. And I think about how a child is a wild animal, about another person carrying your heart forever. My husband got fed up, decided he'd had enough, closed the telescope and took it to the garage to store with his tools, my father-in-law's tractor, and the canoe and paddles. The little man, as my in-laws call him, wasn't crying, and it was so silent in his bedroom that I had to poke him to see if he was still alive. I went back into the room with the patio doors, walked straight towards my reflection, and slid the door open just before I crashed through. My husband was smoking another cigarette, he'd started a second pack while insulting the moon, women and me in equal parts. I saw the smoke surround him and felt afraid. The most aggressive thing he'd said to me in seven years was 'Go and get yourself checked out'. I'd said to him 'You're a dead man' during the first month of our relationship. We were standing side by side in the freezing cold, the water in the grass dyeing us. Our feet soaking wet. The earth churned into craters by the moles. He wasn't looking at the sky any more, and neither was I, of course. But I thought a meteor passed above us, fleeting like everything else in life. Later, we went to sleep, each in our own bed. I'd already grown used to sleeping alone, stretched out diagonally across the bed in this house that was once a dairy farm, whatever that might mean. Any old group of people can make up a family, I said suddenly, letting my eyes wander.

When my husband's away, every second of silence is followed by a hoard of demons infiltrating my brain. A rat jumps onto the see-through roof. She seems to be enjoying herself, the crazy little thing. Every minute or so I go and check the baby's still breathing. I touch him to see if he responds, uncover him, change his position, shine a light on him, pick him up. He's still at the age when cot death is a risk. Then I get a hold of myself, make a sandwich and sit down in front of the TV. But right away, the aghh, aghh of an owl, that genital sound, involuntary and erotic, terrifies me. I turn off the TV and imagine an orgy of animals, a stag, a rat and a wild boar. I laugh, but then the jumble of creatures is suddenly frightening. The legs, wings, tails and scales tangled up and racing towards pleasure. How does a wild boar ejaculate? I hear the aghh, aghh again, like a man being hanged, aghh, aghh, a hoarse, cat-like gargle coming from the owl's curved beak. Through the patio doors, I can see out to where the old camper van sits. I don't know why, but this vehicle that's left us stranded in the middle of the road on more than one occasion must be cursed. It's covered in rust, but my man says it's still got a few miles left on it and the three of us could drive to the seaside. I worry it'll overturn and that'll be it, bye bye baby. We'll have killed the child between the two of us. Between two and four in the morning it's hardest, later it gets easier and I make myself something to eat. But between two and four I feel this urge to throw myself around. I see the doorknob turn on its own. See myself walking to the woods and leaving the buggy on a downhill slope. Aghh, aghh then thank goodness the phone rings. How far away are you, my love? Still a hundred and seventy miles to go? Oh, you went to McDonald's? And filled up the tank? Right, give me a call from the next service station then. Kiss. Kiss. The quick roadside calls break up my madness. I go back to see if my baby's sleeping. I organise his action figures in order of their arrival in our lives. Will my darling husband head to a cheap hotel with some girl working at the drive-thru? I walk barefoot through the house. I go and leaf through a book. My shelves are full of things I bought for the pregnancy and still haven't read. I'm not good in bed any more and he knows it, I say to myself out of nowhere. That's why he's at some roadside hotel with peeling walls and the vacuous drive-thru girl moving on top of him, bouncing better than I can. I like thinking about sex, not having it. I was always good at the theory and a failure at the practical bit, that's why I don't know how to drive even though I've learnt the traffic laws by heart. I try to concentrate on a book by Virginia Woolf, a gift from my husband, but I'm too full of milk. Why does he sleep so much? Why doesn't he stir? The death of a child is science fiction. I go and check on him. Then I step outside and a red Ferrari speeds by. I stand at the front gate, phone in hand. Apparently the radiation from mobile phones causes cancer. My hand is a terminal case. He'll be calling any second now, like he always does when he gets to the next service station. Melisa, the single mum with two children who lives next door, has left the window open and the light on. I think she's crying, or moaning. She earns a living showing off her arse. A man somewhere will be chatting her up online, typing 'Jesus, you're so hot' and paying more cash to look at her crack for a little longer. Why won't the phone ring? The client wants to lick her, she spreads herself open, the guy's sucking on the monitor in his city-centre flat. I look at the little mongrel tied up across the road, sticking its tongue out at me. It's ringing!

Hi, my love… Hiya! Hi! Did you get a coffee from the machine? What did you have to eat? Okay, I'll wait up for you. Me too. Bye. Kiss. Kiss. There, he's called now. I used the right voice to talk to him. I asked him the same things as always, like what did you have to eat? Why do we women ask our husbands what they ate? What the hell are we hoping to find out by asking what they ate? If they've slept with someone else? If they're unhappy with us? If they're planning to leave us one day when they say they're going out for an ice cream? I dodge the nettles and walk down to the woods. At one point a stag appears and shoots me a hard, animal stare. No one's ever looked at me like that before. I'd put my arms around him if I could. Later on, I read a few pages. Ever since the pregnancy I've been a slow reader and it's only getting worse, one page and I drift off. But what's that faint, broken sighing sound? The neighbour with dyed-red hair showing her hole to another punter or the dog in heat? Waiting for my man is torture. I should cook something for when he gets home but I'm not sure I want to. He's always telling the same story. The time my in-laws were here for the day and I made lunch. The menu: rice croquettes with rice. And they all laugh at me. Well, not all of them, the baby doesn't. But before the baby existed it was all of them. Fits of laughter. Sometimes I want him to cry so I can sneak into bed next to him guilt-free and drain my tits. On days when my husband's not here I get aggressive. I go after the weak, like the fat nurse who comes to give anticoagulant injections to the sick man next door. This woman arrives in her little white car every morning at seven on the dot. Her movements are always the same. She turns off the engine, gets out of her car and walks towards the house as only a government employee or home-care nurse can in a nowhere town like this one. Today I took out the rubbish on the hour and gave her a look of disgust as I walked past. She said hello the way civilised people do and I snarled back. I raised my voice and took a few steps towards her, prepared for a fist fight. She shrank back. Poor plump little nurse, she must have thought I was a refugee from some war-torn country. My hair was a mess and I was wearing one of my man's old basketball shirts, which gave me a figure I don't have. She must have thought I was going to head-butt her and knock her teeth in. No wonder she scurried away into the sick man's house, the little scaredy-cat, to rub him with alcohol and give him his injection. I also act haughty with the cashier ladies at the supermarket, the pizza delivery men and the manicurists. I yell at them in public. I like to make a scene, humiliate them, show them how cowardly they are. Because that's what they are: chickens. How come none of them have tried to fight me? How come none of them have called the authorities to have me deported? It's so obvious they're right, that I'm the one who's looking for trouble, that they're just doing their jobs and not bothering anyone. When my husband goes away in the middle of summer I leave a plastic doll on the back seat of the car and wait for the alarmed neighbours and state employees to come running. I love watching them react like the good citizens they are, like heroes who want to smash the window and save the little one from suffocating. It's fun to see the fire engine arrive in the village, its siren sounding. Morons, all of them. And if I want to leave my baby in the car when it's forty degrees out with the heat index, I will. And don't tell me it's illegal. If I want to opt for illegality, if I want to become one of those women who go around freezing their foetuses, then I will. If I want to spend twenty years in jail or go on the run, then I won't rule those possibilities out either. The other day, the silly blonde down the road told the nurse that in town, but on the other side of the river, some guy had *sexually assaulted* a girl. Then the conversation carried on as if nothing had happened. Only I could have chosen to raise my son in

11

this zoo of punk-rock acid-heads covered in bruises from accidental falls and clichés of self-harm. Personally, I think if your husband or father beats you up it's your call to tough it out. You should be roaring back at them, not saying good morning. Degenerates. The chit-chat, or rather the solipsism, I've put myself through has paid off. There's the sound of my husband's car. Straight to the front gate with a smile. There he is, pulling up... He steers around a rock, I walk back and forth, I'm impatient for him to get out and kiss me, for the smell of tobacco in his moustache. We kiss. Without tongue, like all married couples. We go inside and he puts down the suitcase full of unsold products and samples. He tidies the stack of boxes and shows me the wads of tens. Four thousand in bills of ten, wow. I help him off with his jacket. I turn on the microwave to heat up his second dinner of the night and sparks fly. I leave the food in for too long and burn myself when I reach for the plate. We sit down at the table. We look at each other and chat. Quote unquote. This doesn't count as looking at each other or chatting. A bit later I see him go outside. He says he needs to piss, that he doesn't know how anyone can piss inside. He's addicted to the outdoors, I've no clue what he thinks is so bloody special about the sky. He likes it when it's blue and he's even happier when there aren't any clouds. Personally, I don't give a damn if I'm under the open sky or shut up in a trunk. The baby finally empties my right tit and then my left one. My husband is watching cartoons, he does this to switch off. I go over and run my hand along his cheek and he complains I've interrupted his yawn. Then we turn off the lights one by one in this home of ours, where everything still smells slightly of leather. I was in the middle of a masturbatory marathon when the aghh, aghh returned and distracted me, aghh. When I went to wash my face, I ran into him. He was as flushed as I was. We barely glanced at each other before going our separate ways.

My last memory of the pregnancy is from Christmas. My husband's whole family had come to stay from towns even more in the middle of nowhere than this one. My stomach was churning, the baby was moving at an abnormal speed, and people had their fingers crossed hoping they wouldn't have to rush off to hospital with me and leave their turkey-and-apple dinner unfinished. I was standing in the living room in front of the fire. I can't remember having done anything in particular to reveal how desperate I was feeling. For some time I'd been containing everything, or so I thought, in a swaying motion that was subtle though inten-sifying, when, suddenly, I was offered a seat and something cool to drink. Since when did sitting down and having some water get rid of the desire to die? Thanks, Grandma. I'm fine though. But they sat me down and brought me the glass of cool water anyway. These people are going to make me lose it. I wish I had Egon Schiele, Lucian Freud and Francis Bacon for neighbours; then my son could grow up and develop intellectually by learning that there's more to the world I brought him into than opening old skylights you can't see out of anyway. As soon as all the others had escaped to their rooms to digest their meals, I heard my father-in-law cutting the grass beneath the snow with his new green tractor and thought that if I could lynch my whole family to be alone for one minute with Glenn Gould, I'd do it. Later on I saw him sitting at his desk, going over last month's supermarket receipts. He read the price of each product and then checked the total with a calculator. By the time he'd finished recording the sums in his log of monthly expenses, the desk lamp was no longer giving off enough light. We ate dinner, all of us together again, and I can still remember the tired, backlit image of an average man who thinks he's exceptional. After that, he cleaned his dentures and went to bed. And this is a day lived? This is a human being living a day of his life? In his bedroom there's a rifle; on his night table, a few cartridges. I won't be killed in my own bed, he says. If I hear noises, I'll load my gun and go downstairs. And if there's trouble, I'll fire. Straight at the feet, he'd say, inhaling the saliva that was always caught in his throat. My mother-in-law watched me all day long, worrying. She didn't know what else to do when she knocked on my door at dawn and entered timidly with another glass of water and a green-and-white pill. Thanks, I said, and as soon as she left I tossed it into the fire. I don't like side effects. I don't like antidepression. The only thing I could do at times like this was hug my womb and wait. The baby was asleep in there, wrapped up in my guts, foreign to me. He wasn't much help back then either. As soon as the ritual of the raised glasses and well-wishing was over, I tried to escape my husband's gaze. He was already throwing darts at the bull's eye on the terrace. Every time he missed a shot he'd say, Arghh! I walked through the living room, which was strewn with wrapping paper, ribbons and other decorations, to the pile of clothes for the unborn child, but I didn't put anything away. Instead I went out into the woods, exhausted from the contractions. When I think back now, the pain returns, leaping onto me like a dog. The questions asked that Christmas perforated me with more force than hunters' bullets. Have you been looking for work? Do you think you'll send the kid to a nursery? Are you paying your taxes? And your health insurance? Do you need any help? I'm finally here. I only ever come down to the woods at night when it's an emergency. How is it possible for my father-in-law to spend the afternoon before Christmas going over receipts with a firearm under his pillow. How is it possible for my mother-in-law to speak so softly, walk so neatly, be so proper, and yet offer Prozac to a mother-to-be. How is it possible for my in-laws to have slept in the same sheets, under the same duvet and bedspread, in the same wallpapered room, for fifty years. My husband put down the darts and went looking for me in the forested fields. I walk on and shut myself away among the clusters of trunks and saplings. I'm one person, my body is two. Through threads of smoke, I see a small group of gypsies off on their own, camping near the snow-covered pond in a caravan as ramshackle as ours. I see them there, on the ice and frost, smoking and laughing in another language. In the morning, my in-laws will complain about the beer cans and needles left lying around. Beyond are the bee hives with wild honey and the path that leads to the main road. Mushrooms sprout up everywhere after a downpour, and now I can see them rotting. I hope the first word my son says is a beautiful one. That matters more to me than his health insurance. And if it isn't, I'd rather he didn't speak at all. I want him to say magnolia, to say compassion, not Mum or Dad, not water. I want him to say dalliance. My husband found me jumping through puddles. I was embarrassed. I said I was just fine and ran back home.

My first memory of the baby outside me is from the porch of my house. Night is falling and so it begins: the decline, the anxiety, the descent into an altered state. I'm afraid of the harm I could cause the newborn, that's why I'm sitting here in the wicker chair counting fireflies or the cries of animals. I don't join the others at the table when they call me to eat – leftovers, still, from the Christmas holidays – or sit with them when they're gathered by the fire the way they are now. I hear forks entering mouths and food being swallowed as I begin to lose my mind, though I don't know if that's really what's happening. No one does. Not me, not my man, certainly not any doctor. My mother-in-law is addicted to doctors, I need only sneeze and she's ready to call one. She loves them, idolises them. I bet she gets wet even saying the word. I don't know what she thinks they can do about her ruined pancreas, though. My mind is spent, it's lost on the river bank. When I finally go in, the food will be cold on the counter and there'll be a note in his writing saying 'Enjoy your dinner, I love you'. By the end of the night, I've built up so much rage that I could drink until I have a heart attack. That's what I tell myself but it's not true. I couldn't even down half a bottle. My days are all like this. Endlessly stagnant. A slow downfall. Now my mother-in-law is serving dessert, the spoon scraping the bottom of the bowl. Pears baked in brandy, or covered in chocolate. They no longer ask why I don't sit with them. Why I don't share the bed, or the table, or the bathroom. Sometimes I go out to kick at the air, and even if I saw my in-laws spying on me through the window I wouldn't stop. I've already counted three fireflies and there must be more. From out here, I can see it everywhere and that's why I don't go in. Death is present in the fire, in the carpet, in the curtains, in the stuffiness of the old furniture and the silverware. In the flowerless vase. Death seeps out of the umbrellas piled up near the door. I lie down and get up so many times that I don't know when I did what. The baby's so small he gets lost among the sheets, like a tiny fish. Everyone will wear black, even the children. The night is scaring me. I'd put Glenn Gould on in the background to make myself feel better but classical music sends my husband to sleep. It knocks me out, darling, he says. The fact that my father-in-law died in his sleep doesn't help. The sky is like a velvet stage curtain that stops us seeing what's behind it. However hard I try, it just closes me out further. His last words before going to bed – 'My grandson will follow in my footsteps' – were meant as nothing more than a sweeping platitude, but they only make matters worse. As I stood in front of his grave, a sudden, perfect image of his teeth came to me. He was always either complaining that they hurt or picking food out from between them as he spoke. I noticed some people, only a few, on the other side of the grave tearing up. Others felt obliged to keep a respectful distance from the body. He's gone. He's now a man who's passed. That's that. Like a horse trotting through a town and no one even remembering the clatter of its hooves. I hug my husband and our baby smiles at the graves. I thought about my mother-in-law opening up the house to air it out. Throwing away her dear husband's spectacles, smelling him on the backrest of the rocking chair where he used to doze. My sweet little mother-in-law. Cooking for herself, from now on, with the same pans she used for his fried eggs and porridge. Giving her husband's socks away to the neighbours who have the same size feet. While they lower him down in his coffin, I see her going from the bathroom to the bed, I hear him speak, cough, snore. I see her nightgown revealing her dark purple nipples and swollen ankles. My mother-in-law covering her mouth with her hand, clinging to her husband's bedpan. My mother-in-law in slow motion, an elderly woman gasping for air after sliding a door shut or closing a skylight. She tells the family that her husband squeezed her hand tight just before he died, but that the doctor said it had only been a reflex reaction. It was then that I felt close to her for the first time.

Now I'm speaking as him. As him, I think of her and my mouth goes dry. I don't know what she's doing lying on her back in the thick, light grass, tossed aside like a piece of junk. She's wearing the same shirt she had on yesterday. Pink, sleeveless. The same black trousers she had on last week. He sees everything: I recognise every piece of clothing in her wardrobe by now, he says to himself. She has wellies on even though it's not raining. She wears flared skirts to give herself curves, but they disappear as soon as she puts on denim shorts. She ties her hair up in a tight bun like an imitation classical ballerina about to walk on stage. I know her positions off by heart. She sits hunched over, her head hanging between her legs. Or she lies down, like now, as if someone's just dumped her there and forgotten about her. She eats with her hands, straight from the pan, but only when she's alone. She winds handkerchiefs around her neck like a Burmese woman does metal coils. Her bra straps show. I can't smell her and I can't tell if she's breathing heavily. I don't know what it feels like to touch her back. I'm missing the details. The closest I came was the time I drove my motorcycle up to her front gate, but the sound of the engine scared her and I had to drive off. Did she look at me? Does she ever think about me? Her eyes are what intrigue me most, not knowing exactly what colour they are. I'd say they're grey, but sometimes they seem closer to the colour of hay. What would it be like to have her eyes fixed on mine? I know she has broad shoulders and her fingers are slender. I know she almost never laughs, that she walks with such large strides it's as though she's marching in a military parade. She doesn't smoke. Or at least I've never seen her smoke. She doesn't listen to music, at least not in the late evening just before nightfall when I stop by after work, my mouth already dry half an hour before I mount my motorcycle and put on my helmet. Half an hour before knowing that I'll see her sitting on the swing with her baby, blonde like her. Frail and long. Throwing him up into the air and grabbing him clumsily on the way down. Though once she missed. I'll see her cry, see her fury in the way she holds her mouth. I don't know her name or her age. I don't know anything at all. I heard her singing opera in a deep baroque voice once and it's obvious she wasn't born here, but where was she born, and when? If someone had told me this story at work, I wouldn't have believed it. A man like me. The person in charge of the X-ray department at the city's health clinic. A radiologist who graduated from the public university, class of '83. Married with a daughter who's different, who has special needs. An easy-going guy, a man of the house. Born and raised in the city closest to here. A man who spent all his childhood and teenage years in the same flat in the same region in the centre of the country. Spellbound by a woman who wears flared skirts and spends her afternoons sprawled out like an amphibian on her lawn. I see her for as long as the slowest speed of my motorcycle allows. Those few fatal seconds. I think about her and heave with desire. A man like me, not particularly good, but not the devil either. A man like me who enjoys running his fingers through his wife's soft hair, who makes love to her slowly, respecting her moods and her menstrual cycle, and only when our little girl's asleep. A sharp, fun guy who doesn't overcomplicate things. And now the hazard lights are on and I've pulled up on the side of the road. I'm hounded by this dryness in my mouth, knowing that on my way home I'll pass her front gate and see her there among the flowers. Those images that will then last the ten miles separating her from my house. Furious images stuck to my palate. Her among the thorns, a dream-like orange vision, and me a crazy fox on the roadside. The farms and animal pens pass by, first I hear clucking and then I see the chicken coop. The same people as always say hello with their hands in the earth or on a cow's udders or holding some shears up in a tree. This familiar setting with its farm equipment, cow dung, poultry houses and hunting dogs is spoilt by the image I drag home with me like a piece of rubbish. The image that grows inside me, causing chaos. The horror of this desire. Wanting to skin, to flay, to escape what pursues me. I wave to my beautiful wife who's pulling up weeds with her garden gloves, but the image continues to follow me when I park and go inside. An aura expanding. My tree, insipid and leafless, becomes voluptuous. And she's with me when I hold my daughter in my arms. Even when I put food in her little mouth and bathe her. And beyond. Far beyond. Today at dawn I cried for her on the kitchen floor, pounding the tiles with my fists and longing to have her finger bones, her hips, the flesh of her buttocks here with me. I fooled myself believing this was the lowest I could go. An image poisons you: the eyes of an owl, and just like that, it's too late. I push her up against the wall, undo her bun with my teeth and strangle her with my kisses.

What would you like us to do with your ashes? she asked her husband when his lungs were giving out. Eh? he replied, his hearing almost gone. Do you want us to bury you, dear, or scatter your ashes? She had to shout. I don't care, he answered. He wasn't interested in leaving final instructions about that or anything else. My mother-in-law, who carried on washing her husband's trousers when he was gone, relived his death day after day. Her house was a big block of solid concrete with a view of the open fields of dry pasture and corn beyond a row of vegetable gardens. The paved path leading to it was dirty, the air tainted with carcinogenic smoke. Someone was burning copper cables to resell. The moles dug deep holes in what was also their land, turning it into a minefield. My father-in-law used to say definitive action needed to be taken by putting gas bottles at the entrance to their homes: the Shoah of moles. She went on cooking for two, changing the pillowcases, mending his underwear that was torn at the crotch. In the morning, still awake from the night before, I'd go by with the buggy and see her sitting there, in a daze, her head inside a bell. She lived in her body as though it were an infested house, as if she had to tiptoe through it trying not to touch the floor. The only time she was at peace, she said, was in her sleep, when the spirit scatters. But she had serious difficulty sleeping and used to sleep-walk. Once she strolled through the village in a nightie shouting *Fire!* Another time she used a shoe as a phone and conversed with God by means of it. This was when she wasn't doing the hoovering at four in the morning. I saw her breakfast consisted of white bread that had been left out in the kitchen for days. She didn't check the expiry date on the medication she started taking the day of the funeral. She didn't scare away the flies or remove the eggs they'd laid in the jar of homemade chestnut jam. She watched the fingers bringing the bread to her mouth as though they belonged to someone else and she choked, because time doesn't pass for the person who's left behind. It's a perpetual limbo. Like a wet shirt, clammy against the body, something that doesn't go away, that won't come unstuck. And although her life partner had never been one to spend long hours embedded inside her, entire afternoons, summers, clinging to her, nor days in the countryside entering her, satiating her; although he didn't even consider whether or not she got aroused (she was that hollow, that bare), he'd been her companion nevertheless. Instead of a vagina, he thought his wife had a stone in the depths of a cave. He always imagined her covered in the little shawls she embroidered. He got used to loving her as though she'd been born that way. And she got used to being loved that way. When she saw her husband's washed corpse she was shocked because before it turned to ash, it had the shape of a body born in the autumn of 1940. And it, and his pedantry, his monologues from the head of the table, his laughter from atop the tractor he drove, all ended up locked in a pinewood coffin. As did the little secrets, the visits to the local brothel, the time his roving hand found its way under the skirt of a secondary-school student on the bus and it was the talk of the town. In it, too, went the heroic exploits from his time in the navy, the deaths he tracked with marks in his groin, the game of cards in a train carriage at the age of thirty-two and the time he made her laugh so hard she wet herself and had to hurry off to change. It was a run-of-the-mill wake, a quick goodbye. An excellent father and husband, said the guests. Better than excellent. The procession then made its way to eat at the inn where the dead man had been a regular. He was there every lunchtime, drinking his beer and his aperitifs, telling witty tales of his time on the front line. The guests remembered him as a man among comrades, but his widow revealed that he used to sit for hours in the semidarkness of the living room facing the lit-up tree. And it wasn't so much my father-in-law's death that affected me, but rather the loss of his words, *In all my born days*, his turns of phrase, *Well, I happen to be rather good at that*, and his thick, spit-filled tone. So much screwing around, so many memories of bravery from the war, so much debauchery, but in the end no one really had anything to say about him.

The night was high, black and smooth above us. An unwelcoming, pretentious darkness. The fan was rotating. My wonder-daughter was dreaming inside the white netting, soft as a fish with no scales. I was obsessed with sleeping. My wife had been dreaming away by my side for hours and the mosquito coils had disintegrated, leaving behind the smell of teenage holidays. I got up and tiptoed to the door, taking with me the clothes that were hanging on the back of the iron chair. I got dressed in the darkness of the hallway, carried my shoes to the door and tied my laces below the open sky. It wasn't until I'd pushed my motorcycle a block away that I got on and started the engine. I saw the trees that had been chopped down by a single blow from an axe. I saw the rabbit skulls riddled with holes, scattered like flowers at the entrance to the woods. I saw a cluster of nocturnal butterflies that fluttered around my head, into my ears and under the collar of my shirt. They gradually got tangled in my hair and flew up my nose. The fresh air coming off the hill and the road didn't take away the feeling I had of being smothered. I rode on along the motorway, passing peaceful men carrying rifles and machetes. I was getting closer to her in large leaps. I passed the houses that came before hers. The house with the boarded-up windows, the one with the fake roses outside, the one with the twin Siberian huskies. I turned off the engine, left the motorcycle leaning in the grass and moved towards her front gate. I walked there and back, seeing and not seeing into her garden and house. All I could make out through the foliage were fragments. Then a light pierced the pitch darkness. Someone had just woken up. Or was it the baby, shaken by the images in his dreams. I put my hand on the gate latch and set foot in her territory for the first time. Her house standing before me looked like a landscape. My shoes flattened the earth. I took a few steps forward, careful not to be seen from either of the two small front windows. I ran my hand along the wall that was cracked as though by lightning, and made my way round to the back of the house. The light was still on but nothing more than the aggressive shhh of the barn owl could be heard. I was expecting to see her come down through the air in a white nightdress, possessed by spirits. I was expecting to see her appear in the window with red eyes. Or floating above the roof dressed all in black. There, in her space, I could feel the hatred that dug at her womb and I begged not to be infected by the depression she felt at having to live. Because she's infectious, the bitch. Infectious and so beautiful. Another window opened. A sudden gash in the wall. Too scared to run away, I stayed put and waited for something to happen. For her husband to come out or a dog to bite me. Or for her to appear, which would be more frightening still. Then I heard creaking thumps on a wooden staircase. Her feet were metal talons. Her long hair hanging down to the floor was made of particles. I stood there like a statue with wet feet. She appeared. She rode the wind towards me but was pulled back by a strong gust. Suspended in mid-air, she opened her glorious mouth as if to scream but nothing came out. I could hardly restrain myself. I found her irresistible the way she was, even though she was a few steps away from the septic tank. Despite my violent lust, despite my desire to gobble her up, to inhale her, I didn't move. Neither did she. I'd say that was when we met for the first time, there among the shadows. In that instant, we shared the tragedies of our lives. That was us talking about the past, about why we were in this pit, this insect-infested hole, and why we were running away in the middle of the night. Grab a knife and slice your lip open, she told me. I obeyed while she galloped into the house, and even with her back turned she was watching me bleed. I escaped on my motorcycle, waking everyone up.

I'm at the table after dinner. The meal has been cleared away and all that's left is my glass. The plates are drying on the rack, the salt is in its place and my husband has gone to lie down. The new dog is about to piss somewhere. I know I have to get up, but I don't. I stretch my legs out onto another chair and nod off while sucking on a toothpick. Now the dog's coming to piss under the table but I still don't get up. My trousers are unbuttoned. From here I can take in the view of the fields opening up to the horizon. I can see each of the round bales of hay. I must have eagle eyes. I can see not only the shadows of the trees, the way they're drawn, but also the parasites that cling to the trunks. I can see into the ground and make out the creatures that live there while we sleep. Cows float down the river at this time of day, their stiff legs poking up into the air. They don't expect the current to be so strong when they bend down to drink. These bovine corpses look like rocks or men when you see them from the suspension bridge. The still-unnamed dog tugs at the tablecloth and breaks my glass. It's finally pissing and its snout is all red. We should give it a name. Personally I'd have no problem calling it Dog, but my husband's insisting on giving it a proper name and making it part of the family. I need to take a piss too, though I still haven't moved and am cramping up. Something I always used to hate about living in the countryside, and that I now relish, is that you spend all your time killing things. Spiders appear in the sink as I'm having my morning coffee, and they drown as soon as I turn on the tap. The stronger ones manage to resist for a while, folding into themselves like tight little flowers. They're the ones that provoke me to run the hot water to destroy them. The flies' turn comes when I'm spreading the quince jelly. They've been following us around since prehistoric times and it's about time they died out. I trap them in the jar with a swift twist of the lid, then sit with the baby on my knee and watch them slide around in the jelly. Sitting comfortably on the swing, I electrocute bees and teach the wasp that wants a piece of me a lesson. My son and I stuff clusters of ants into matchboxes and then set them on fire. They must give off a good smell because he takes a deep breath in. I don't smell a thing. Later on I stamp on worms and grasshoppers, but my favourite of all is leaving little cups of beer on the terrace, not too full, so the brown slugs have to climb in to take a sip. When I walk by at night, I find a whole gathering of drunken slugs, in the liquid, around the container and even underneath it. In the bathroom, sitting on the toilet, I like to take the broom and clear the cobwebs from the ceiling in one fell swoop. The dog's finished pissing. I refuse to wipe it up. I never wanted to adopt this dog, it was my husband who took pity when we saw it lying in the middle of the road on the way back from the supermarket. The puddle of piss reaches all the way to the door and underneath it. The dog goes licking its way along until it reaches the slippers of its master, who's just woken up. Obsequious boot-licking dog. Indoctrinated dog. What's all this, says the husband, alarmed at the sight of piss and broken glass. I'm not surprised: I'd be alarmed if I were him, but instead I'm me and I haven't even got up. He walks round the table, takes a good look and starts asking questions. I know, I say. What do you know? Don't make me say it. If I'm saying I know, that should be enough. Well, actually it isn't. What are you doing just sitting there? Can't you see the pup's pissing itself, the poor thing? Can't you see you're stepping on glass? Why are your trousers undone? I felt sorry for him, married to someone whose trousers were undone. Is that not allowed? I ask. You know perfectly well this has nothing to do with your trousers! I'll wear my trousers unbuttoned if I want to! Come here, he says, opening his arms. No. Come here. No. Why not? Because. What should I do, sweep this up? Do what you want. Are you staying there, then? Yep. You could be doing a better job taking care of the house. Do you know what I found in the kitchen behind the gas cylinder? A dried-up rat and some worms. How long has our baby been eating food cooked on that stove? And what about you? I retort. You can stop dropping your ash in the mugs and on the plates, for one thing. How long has our son been eating off them? Well, buy some ashtrays then! He goes outside, the dog following submissively behind, and I hear the creature let out the rest of the piss still trapped in its bladder. He gets the broom and comes back to clean up, trying not to hurt me, nudging the dog away with his foot. I keep staring at the empty table. There's no trace of dinner. It's a universal truth that at this time of day, when the light changes and things start to decline, objects either get cleared away or they get broken. Let's go outside, love. What for, love? It's too stuffy in here, love. It's stuffy out there as well. He looks at me and then leaves. I know I have to get up, that this time I have no choice. But just like when I dig my fingernail into my gums so they swell, I go on sitting in the chair, my limbs cramping up, knowing I'm face-to-face with something that's disintegrated. That dinner, that time we spent eating less than an hour ago, a family portrait showing various generations, seven siblings standing on a staircase smiling, all of them now dead. I sit there, stuck, unable to move, as if I were behind a door, waiting to be let in. I heard the car engine snort into action and realised it was an ultimatum. My hands moved violently, as though they might break into pieces, and yet I stayed there long enough for my husband to overheat the engine and say, ...therfucker! I got up, stiff. The car was running and the dog was in the back seat. My husband flashed the lights at me. I left the front door open and went over to the car window. The dog's filthy paws are all over the baby's car seat, do something! It'll move them soon, get in. Don't make me go for a drive. I'm not fucking around! We need to talk. Things can't go on like this. You have no idea about anything, I think he said, or wanted to say. I wasn't clear-headed enough to argue either. It was cold, the cold you feel when it's no longer two or three in the morning but four or five. The baby, I said. The baby's fine, I'm the one who's not. Whenever he said that, I knew he was furious. I bit my tongue and got in. The dog was mucking up the baby's seat, using it as a bed inside the car. Soon after that we're driving through the next town, listening to rock songs on the local radio despite the terrible reception. The early-morning mist is hiding the roofs, stables and wineries, and covering the sleeping animals, milking yards and churches like a murky veil. My husband starts to hum and whistle along to a song in English. Great tune, he says, and turns up the volume. The Smiths. To him, I might as well be from another planet because I've never heard of them. Because I think only morons listen to rock. Because I don't find guitars exciting. The dog is sleeping, snout between its paws. During the chorus, *And when a train goes by, it's such a sad sound. No... it's such a sad thing,* his hands came up off the wheel and he barely managed to slam on the brakes. A stag hit the windscreen. First its head, then its body took off to the left of the car, like some kind of flying creature. There was a huge dent in the bonnet. The dog whimpered. My upper body shot forwards. I always forget to wear my seatbelt. Though we'd been going slowly, I hit my forehead against the glove compartment and was left feeling dazed. You could have really hurt yourself! I've told you a thousand times, always wear your seatbelt! Everyone okay? and he turned around to the excited, panting dog that was fogging up the windows. But then he saw its leg, swaying disobediently to the rhythm of the windscreen wipers as though it were scratching its hip. We got out of the car, my husband with the dog in his arms. The music was still playing. The dog licked its beaten body. The stag ran off as best it could, limping, as though it didn't understand it had survived. My husband looked at the damaged radiator, then remembered about me and gave me a hug. The heavy smoke coming out of the car blinded us and for a second he kissed the dog on the mouth and I kissed the trunk of a fallen tree. We'll have to push, he said, but first he walked a few feet away and lowered his tracksuit bottoms. I have an obscene husband. How can you take it out at a time like this? Now what, he said, like someone chewing gum at a funeral. The animal did the dirty work, licking the remains off the bonnet, shaking its head once the job was done. We christened it Blood, in English, but ended up calling it Bloody. We wrapped it up in whatever we could find, put it in the back of the car and fastened the seatbelt. I pushed while my husband accelerated and then I ran to catch up with the moving car. I had to run so hard I thought they were trying to leave me behind. At home, I found the baby standing up, his hands sticking through the bars of the crib, screaming for the prison warden. My man was already rinsing the car off with the hose. The dog followed him around with a pained look on its face like it couldn't bear it any more, its eyes watering, its leg dragging, its body writhing as it made holes in the ground. We went to sleep. Bloody's cry, eeeeee, eeeeee, echoed throughout the house. It was driving me crazy. I got up, grabbed the small torch from the tool drawer and went into the garage. I rummaged through everything. Layers of filth had accumulated on the pieces of wood, on the unused furniture and the swivel chairs; only the telescope seemed clean, sheathed as it was in clear plastic. I knew I'd regret it if I left it at that. I went outside, leaving the front door open. The cold air would chill the house in no time. In wellies and half-naked, I went to my mother-in-law's place. I wasn't out in the countryside, I was in a spaghetti western. I found the rabbit-paw keyring hidden in the flowerpot next to her front door and let myself in. If my father-in-law had been alive, he'd have fired, no matter the direction, just for the pleasure of pulling the trigger. The pile of ironed shirts, the books organised on the shelves, nothing gave the impression that someone had recently died. I went up the suspended staircase, holding onto the ropes on either side. My mother-in-law was asleep, doped up. She was a plank, her eyes covered by a mask, two pieces of cotton-wool in her ears; a flat-chested, sexless body like a table wrapped up in sheets. Next to her were a piano and a Japanese drawing of a small island. Her bedroom was snow. She didn't even blink when I made a noise tripping over the long laces of her shoes. I lit a candle and looked at the piano again, feeling an urge to play a note. I searched. Some people need to be able to see the ocean, but I need to be able to see a firearm, even if it's motionless, dirty and unloaded. When my husband opened one eye, he found me aiming at him. He was so scared he couldn't say a word. Kill him, I said. What, kill who? Eeeeee, eeeeee. Kill the dog. Why would I kill him? Because he's suffering. So what? Leave him alone. You can't be serious. Eeee, eeee. We'll call the vet tomorrow, he said, and rolled over onto his side, his arse facing me. Call who? Go on, kill him now, I said, out of my mind. But he didn't even flinch, in fact he let out a snore almost as loud as Bloody's whimpers. I stayed there, watching him sleep, astonished by his relentless

33

cowardice. Shotgun in hand, I went from room to room until I reached the corner of the kitchen where, all twisted on a filthy rag, Bloody was sobbing with pain. I aimed. My brain went blank. I felt like an Israeli soldier and suddenly, in my mind, I heard the order. Fire! Fire, you bastard! And there, for the first time in my life, I pulled the trigger.

On rainy days in the city, people consume films, plays, restaurant meals. Out in the country they tell each other stories, thinking they can fight off the boredom that way. After the wedding, they were on the upper deck of a sleeper bus. They were still dressed as they had been for the party, with glitter in their hair and confetti on their clothes. They'd taken off their shoes, placing hers inside his. They were going on their honeymoon in the south, staying in a cabin on the edge of a lake. 'Looking out onto a mirror' was how the brochure described it. She was sleeping on the shoulder of the man she'd just married. He watched the road come rushing towards him. The skid marks of wheels on tarmac. And the oil stains. And the animals flattened until their fur merged with the pavement. And the clouds that were no longer red but grey. It was cold because of the air-conditioning. His wife had covered herself with his suit jacket and the bus driver was coughing. The man looked at her and then stared at his reflection in the window against the backdrop of the night. At the petrol station, he got off and left her asleep. He asked for a light from the bus driver, who was leaning against the hot bonnet, puffing on a cigarette and blowing the smoke towards the passengers. The man walked around the mildewed station and saw an entire family crouching down and eating among the buses. He also saw some elderly people sleeping on a row of benches, and wondered if they knew each other. He noticed that a large part of the petrol station was in darkness. They hadn't told anyone, and the ruffled dress hid it well, but she was pregnant.

They were pregnant, she'd say. My future husband was being carried in that womb. The man saw that the bus driver was halfway through his cigarette, and walked farther away so it would take him longer to get back. He reached a wooden shed among the weeds, went behind it and unzipped his flies, but nothing came out. He was dry. He could make out a town like a shadow beyond the petrol station. The bus driver stepped on his cigarette butt and cracked his spine, and at that point the man began to hurry back. Buses don't wait. He climbed the vehicle's curving staircase with another passenger who must have been his age but seemed much younger. He looked for his seat, running his hands along the ceiling to keep his balance. She was sleeping as if she were in bed, her mouth half-open. She had her hands on her belly, replicating the abundant gesture of pregnant women everywhere. He got comfortable and again the road came rushing towards him. And the crosses with names of the dead on the roadside. And the rubbish tips with their birds. And the power lines carrying electricity to and fro. And he cried the whole way. First, in front of the churned-up earth of a stretch of wasteland. Then, on a bend in the road that opened onto the sea. Later, upon hearing the gallop of hail on the roof. He cried and cried. When the bus reached the final straight, he was still watching the landscape as it gradually lit up, having barely slept. She stretched, smiled widely and said, Good morning, darling, without moving her hands from the belly that by then contained the seed of what would become my lover. This is the story I heard about my in-laws' honeymoon. This is what will remain for their children, and their children's children, and beyond. A dog crouched defecating by the side of the road sees a bus go past and light up its shit, and a man inside, against the glass, crying.

With one hand I hold my little boy; with the other, I hold a scraper. I prepare the meal with one hand; I stab myself with the other. It's great having two hands. Very practical. They're waiting for me out there with the engine running. I hurry, trying not to trip. They honk the horn. I heard you! They insist I go with them, that I tuck myself in on the passenger side, seatbelt nice and tight, all set for the Sunday outing. Where to? says my mother-in-law, who's no longer mourning and now acts like any other widow, one of the many who sit at tables in modern-looking cafés eating pastries. Where do you want to go? she asks and it's always the same. It seems I can't just stay quiet, just stare out of the window. No, I have to come up with a destination. We could go for aperitifs and chips by the river, watch the old-timers water-ski by in their wetsuits. We could go to the city, climb the steps up to the bell tower in single-file and, like tourists who marvel at the most ridiculous things, gaze enraptured at a stone or the red rooftops of the houses. We could go to the country fair, or have coffee in town near the market that reeks of roasting meat. Must appear enthusiastic, must show others we enjoy life. Must take the child here, there and everywhere, buy him balloons, let him ride on the merry-go-round to nowhere, take pictures of him, because that's how you give your child a childhood. I don't mind where we go, but let's get a move on! says my mother-in-law with a widow's zeal. She's only just begun to cut her nails again, to sleep through the night without feeling for the dead man's body, to eat breakfast without sobbing into her milky coffee. And, of course, she wants to go for rides. Her only child takes his old mother out of this sewer, and it does her a world of good. I notice we're crossing the suspension bridge. My husband wants me to take the wheel and practise driving up in the hills, but I don't feel like it. It makes me dizzy. Below, there are sand dunes and families sitting in folding beach chairs. There are grandparents on their day off from the nursing home, pleased as can be to spend time with their children and grandchildren. There are a few depressed pregnant women hiding their cigarettes, and the odd rehabilitating heroin addict. There are all kinds of people. That's where my mother-in-law wants to go. We park on a slope and my man pulls the handbrake and leaves the car in first gear so we don't end up under the bridge. Here we are, one more family going out to watch the sunset. As though we had no idea that the sun came up and went down again. I mean, seriously, it does this every day. The baby crawls around and my mother-in-law follows behind with a sore back. I get bored watching a swan floating along, keeping its head above water, biting on stems and aquatic plants, and then going for the neck of a dog in a boat (it used to be so graceful, that dog, back when it had a neck…). Suddenly, something breaks the monotony. A wave of people churns up the coast, a murmur is rising. The people crowd together, moving closer to the river. I see a police car crossing the bridge, then two or three more. It's like we're all here for a firework display. People pile up, we're all part of the same family now. It turns out that a gay thirteen-year-old has said farewell on Twitter and come here to throw himself off the bridge. He thanked his followers for their support beforehand. The police call in the fire-fighters, but they're all as useless as each other. They put up blue-and-white police tape, which of course does nothing to keep people away. Even my baby is curious and I let him look.

But I don't want to waste my time watching some corpse floating on the water. It might give everyone a shock now, a rush of adrenaline, but the time will come when the living and the dead will be indistinguishable. That subtle difference of being, barely noticeable to a lorry driver who passes a man taking a siesta by the roadside or one who's recently been run over. A difference the lorry driver would struggle to make out between one man lounging in the sun and another in the same position who's just had a stroke. A lovely Sunday was had by all.

Above me the turquoise of rusted bronze, the autumnal earth rotating, sleep interrupted. I get dressed, still not fully awake, because I just heard him. I leave the house barefoot and move like an animal to the gate, and I don't go back. His presence is my mouth's desire made flesh. It is longing for lightning and watching the sky answer you. It is asking for the texture of white sand and seeing the town become a beach. It is wishing for a horse and having one walk slowly by, brushing against you with his back. The bucolic surroundings, the little gate leading to the pond, the fruit fallen from trees, a swamp; it all becomes arousing. Insipid things really go to my head. He's standing in front of the fence that surrounds my house. I look at him while he looks at me, and I know that afterwards I'll go out into the woods and vomit everywhere. I look at him and know that afterwards I'll have a beak, feathers, talons. At first, as often happens at first, I don't know if I should kick him out or stick a rake into his chest, but then, as if firing silver sparks into the black air, we kiss. My husband was sleeping and the baby was falling out of bed. A pebble that slips off a cliff.

Everything had two simultaneous beginnings: the first, a toxic dream, and the second, the condoms found in the car's glove compartment, melted by the sun of the infernal summer that just ended. The whole thing played out with sermons, questions and evidence. We beat each other's brains out, pecked at each other's heads like birds in a cockfight, while military planes did drills in the air above us. Training for a war that was already ending. Every so often one of them would turn in on itself and I'd imagine its wing embedded in my cheekbone. Yesterday I dreamt I found you in bed with the neighbour and I never remember my dreams. I cried all morning, he says. Is that so. Well, I found condoms in the glove compartment, what were they doing there? You don't think the car's a good place to fuck. You're not answering my question. That's because you didn't ask a question. I told you about my dream. Are you saying it meant nothing? I don't know what neighbour you're talking about. The one who showed up in the middle of the night, the one who drives by every day on his damned motorcycle. I don't know. They say you should deny everything, even when faced with the evidence. If it comes to it, I'll deny who I am. What's his problem, what does he want? What does who want? Next time I'll go out and ask him myself then, we'll see what he wants. I've got my suspicions too, who doesn't. What suspicions, about what? Just tell me who he is. No one, I said, my back already turned. But I felt his gaze like a kitchen knife on my throat each time he came closer. Don't take me for an idiot. And I kept saying I didn't,

I didn't, but his black hair had already poisoned me. Typical. Us women, barefoot, naked, entering and closing ourselves in. A private wood that wraps us in its foliage. I won't get angry, I just need to know. But what could I tell him? What is there to say? That he entered me like a snake enters a crocodile's mouth? Like a snake devours a bird, gorging on it slowly, irrevocably? He made space for himself with one slash of a machete. But am I about to tell him that? Once inside, he heard the echo of my voice. And from within my darkened body, he killed me. He must have realised I was having some bad thoughts, because he grabbed hold of my arm in one clumsy movement and stuck a fingernail into my flesh. You're hurting me, I said, plagiarising a diva's pitiful wail. Tell me what's going on! But no one ever wants the truth. Nothing's going on. You're a two-faced liar. Just tell me if you're sleeping with him and I'll leave you alone, I swear! And then the boring speech about jealousy, the blah blah blah that simultaneously destroys the person who's jealous and the person making them jealous, gave way to kicks, blows, idiot, piece of shit, crazy bitch, and other banalities. Until I ran outside, and for the very first time I crashed straight through the glass. Red all over, I crossed the pastures as though they were a park, trampling on rabbits and barn owls as I went. Or were they trampling on me? And I lay down in my kennel, my cave among the pruned trees. I think my husband must have started looking for me but then got tired and nodded off. I remained sprawled on the ground, my socks wet, and cold, dried blood stuck to my body. I was beginning to shake. That's how the long night began, looking at the graves until there was sun in the sky. Brushing my hair and sleeping under the reflection of the tombstones. Reading the names of dead people I never knew. That was my life, or it was going to be my life from then on. When I have sex, I celebrate the birthdays of the departed. When I fall in love, like this very minute, as I shake myself, I scatter earth onto a coffin. It doesn't matter whose. And when I masturbate I desecrate crypts, and when I rock my baby I say amen, and when I smile I unplug an iron lung. Hence the kiss. Because after all, since forever and since even before being born, and for the whole time my husband's been shouting with jealous rage, I've been dead.

They've been treating my cuts for days now. I can't see my whole body, but I've got them all over: on my shoulder blades, my chest, my belly, my neck. They're only small cuts. Every time a new nurse comes in, they stand still for thirty seconds and stare at me, making sure I notice. It's not what you think, I say, but whatever. They shine a light on me lying on the hospital bed and remove tiny shards, bits of blades, splinters. Pieces of crystal, tiny mirrors, petals and slivers of glass come out of my body. First a small ulcer, and the next day, or the day after, a tiny sparkle appears. They disinfect me and give me painkillers. They brought me here straight from the field, unconscious. It's the first time I've fainted and been lost to the world. Now I'm supposed to walk slowly, avoid running at all costs and keep my feet raised when I can. I'm going to have the instep of a zebra. Don't pull open your scabs, they tell me. Apparently a lot of patients pick at their wounds. My husband comes in saying *knock knock* and pretends to hide behind the flowers. He kisses me, avoiding the gashes on my face that won't form scabs. I should probably say something and all I can think of is, I didn't touch him, I didn't touch a hair on his head. I don't know what you're talking about, he says. About his head. Not a hair. Fine, he answers, whatever. And what about you? What were those condoms doing there? What is it you need to do so often at McDonald's instead of coming home early to be with us? Nice move, he says. You're learning. He reaches out to stroke me but his hand falls exactly, precisely, on the cut along my neck.

Lying on the lawn, I yanked out clumps of grass, over and over, green and yellow, worms and soil all blending together in my hand. A beautiful palette. For a pretty gruesome painting, that is. I yanked and yanked, frantic. But it didn't calm me down. I ran inside and when I got to the bedroom I threw the old wooden chair at the mirror, wrenched the door off the wardrobe in one movement, and then the shutters off the window with another swipe. My ovaries wring themselves out and there's a blood clot in my knickers that runs down my legs. I don't think I'm pregnant again, it's just pure rage. I run spastically, the cuts pulling tight. I've never done any sports. At school I used to jump off the diving board and sink to the bottom of the pool, not even trying to come back up, while above me they acted out the whole pantomime of panic. My classmates shouting, I hope she drowns, I hope she drowns! Where are they now? I grab the folds of fat still there from the pregnancy, and it occurs to me that the clot is actually a miscarriage, but no, that's not it at all. It's the remains of my body. My husband is cutting down wood next to the baby in the buggy. I hear the chainsaw. The child watches intently as the pieces of wood crack, detach from the trunk and fall. The child watches his mother fall apart, break down. But he smiles when he sees the particles of wood in the air; he thinks they're flakes of dark snow and isn't worried about me. He's pleased to see the preparations for winter. He must think he's got a normal mother to give his first kindergarten drawings to. Beside him, a tree that was once full of life is now fraying. I've never been so far away from him. Tiny conscienceless body.

Tiny ignorant mind. Mummy, i.e. me, runs and leaps from a pit full of rainwater into the tall grasses of the unkempt pastures. My body will remain undiscovered for years and years; it will become forensic evidence. My buffalo breath suffocates me. I could fog up entire panes of glass, the large windows of a castle, cities mirrored in narrow rivers. I'm a beast who breathes slowly and heavily, leaving no air for anyone else. I stare into the night; it's like a locked trunk. An old railway carriage on its way to hell. I search the thick air for the crack that will let me through. What more do you want from me? says my husband. What do you need? Is there anything I can do? And he places a cushion in front of me. But a cushion won't do it. I punch the air. He runs off and returns with a pair of red boxing gloves he had as a teenager. He puts them on me. I throw two wild cross punches at his nose and then take them off again. I don't want gloves or a boxing ring. I don't want a chest guard. I want to see my hands made of bones firing in every direction. Fuck me, I say in a scream like a bark. Fuck me now! But what I really felt like doing as he came towards me with his hard-on was eat poisonous flowers, poisonous mushrooms, stones. I wanted to put an end to this long, scattered, turbulent day. He threw me onto the bed and the baby was still in the buggy, next to the chopped wood, reaching for the chainsaw. He opened my legs wide. He poked around with his calloused hands. Desire is the last thing there is in my cries. And when his piece of flesh entered my hole (if that's what making love is), I longed for a white room with a sea breeze blowing through it, the salt stinging the cuts on my shredded tongue. Someone heals my eyes, trains my gaze and leaves me in a place infinitely more peaceful than this pigsty. The other man digs around in me, searching. Because there's something to be found. But no one knows how to dig. Not even him. When my husband shrank and pulled out of me, I could feel him throbbing, and although I'd bitten him I loved him. The chainsaw started running.

It doesn't matter if I spent the whole morning wondering how to translate my state of imprisonment. It doesn't matter if I walked the length of the dry, dirty-green riverbed, running through a thousand words in my mind without finding the right one. My mother-in-law stood in the distance with a bowl of chicken feed, complaining that I don't do enough exercise. What is it you do all morning? You could go and take the free yoga class in town. I'd look after him for you. It doesn't matter if your mind drifts to a Shakespeare sonnet, or if you rummage through your consciousness looking for a minute in which you were free and fail to find one. None of it matters. The brain doesn't matter, nor do its reference points and elucubrations, its ways of processing symbols, its eagerness. It only matters what you do, where you go, whether you keep busy. In the end, they're like my neighbours, locked up between unpainted wooden walls. These gypsies who stepped straight out of a brutal universe, one with no morals or laws and far removed from modern shops with electric lighting, pop music, capitalist democracies and the abolition of the death penalty. Melisa is thirty but looks more like fifty. She has a thin mouth closed tight like a slit, and long ginger locks stuck together in clumps that expose the skin of her skull and make her look like a creepy doll. Melisa's twelve-year-old daughter, Jacqueline, lost her virginity in the abandoned house by the lake, that Gothic den, lifting her skirt between drunken moans. No doubt they filled that doe's belly with bones, born and raised as she was in this sordid place full of dingy cafés and people on welfare, the physically disabled and men wearing hand-me-down linen suits and espadrilles. Where were you? What are your plans for tomorrow? What time did you get out of bed? Have you been practising your pronunciation? And your vocabulary? You'll never get through a job interview at this rate. Where are you going? I heard the question as I entered the woods, panting. A mule in labour wouldn't have moved any slower.

And then I saw the air saturated with invisible sexual tension. Rembrandt. The acorns fell and fell and fell so lazily, so heavily between the treetops and the earth that they seemed to be asleep in the air. To be cutting the air with golden rays. Caravaggio. That spell, that somnolence that comes over you as you watch leaves twirl once, twice, a third time before reaching the ground. One leaf falls, then another and another. An atmosphere that leaves you open-mouthed, that turns your saliva into fresh water. Farewell to mould and darkness. The death of summer turned the woods into silence and sighs. With the buggy off to one side of the path, I lay down and slept. I dreamt it was drizzling, but it wasn't. It was the sound of butterfly wings flapping together. That light sensuality of nocturnal butterflies. My heart was beating in my ears. I leaned forwards to look at my baby and forgot that he'd come out of me. Good morning, child of the forest. He looked at the capybaras mating and copied their motions right away with his tiny pelvis. My baby was screwing, an animal like the rest.

Looking him in the eye was the closest I'd come to levitating, if levitating is possible. The stag used to appear at nightfall and linger between the woods and the garden. From the house, you could see his antlers, branching like a menorah. Meeting that gaze is an instant that's still going on. He turned his head, revealing his pupils, and now I'm blind. The child was sprawled on the grass between my feet. Before running off, the stag tossed his head back under the weight of his antlers and opened his big mouth in a U-shape. He seemed to be howling, raving. His mouth was a pit. The baby rolled around and the animal left the scene, but his floating eyes and bellow remained. When everything was dark and there was no in front or behind, I headed back, feeling my way along the grass, the baby clinging onto my hair. His watery nose was dripping on me. I went to wipe both of us clean and ended up treading on an ember that splintered my foot. My husband, tired of my domestic accidents, has put first-aid kits in the bathroom, living room and kitchen. I've already burnt my fingertips, split my skull open, cut my whole body to ribbons. He comes out of the shower, pale and naked. He's hard and he's sad. I don't feel like doing anything, he says, not even watching TV. I flip him off, using my ungainliest finger, and go out through the recently repaired sliding door. I leave the baby sitting by the fire. Looking in at them, I feel like a spider the moment the water hits. I'm freezing cold, but I carry on standing there, watching. My husband grabs a towel, drapes it over the sofa, sits on top and waits to dry off. Little by little he goes soft and his skin takes on its usual orange colour. The baby tries to stand up, using the air for support, and falls back again and again onto his nappy. My face is glued to the glass. I see them grow foggy on the other side of my breath. I see my breath erase them from my life. What happens next is obvious: the baby crawls towards the fireplace and any second now he'll be needing the first-aid kit himself. I bet his father doesn't move. If I'd received all the money I've won in bets over the years, I'd be a millionaire by now. And the winner is… The baby sticks his hands into the embers, his father reacts the way Bush did when he heard about the Twin Towers. I see him run off to look for bandages and anti-inflammatory pills with his stupid towel around his waist. The towel drops and he's not sure how to calm the child who's not screaming or crying, but instead shattering the silence with a kind of snarl. My husband puts TCP on the child's palms and the soles of his feet. His blood looks like foam. He's from outer space. A little red revolutionary child. I don't go in because I'm a stranger, an outsider: I don't know how to speak without causing offence, I spy on people's homes and I haven't showered in days. He's coming towards me, towards the glass, breathing heavily through his nose. I know that when he slides open the door I'll turn into a black swan, and when he starts shouting I'll be a castrated duck. Okay, I'm going in. I'll stop trying to draw blood from a stone. I'll contain my madness, I'll use the bathroom. I'll put my baby to sleep, jerk off my man and postpone my rebellion in favour of a better life. Me, a woman who didn't want to register her son. Who wanted a son with no record, no identity. A stateless son, with no date of birth or last name or social status. A wandering son. A son born not in a delivery room but in the darkest corner of the woods. A son who's not silenced with dummies but rocked to sleep by animal cries. What saves me tonight, and every other night, has nothing to do with my husband's love or my son's. What saves me is the stag's golden eye, still staring at me.

The baby was crying with false convulsions. Water fell from the sky and the chlorine did nothing to stop the pool from rusting. The reflection, more viscous now, sketched out the twisted trees and the parasitic plants that covered them. I tied my baby to my body and we were a kangaroo and her joey hopping around the field of thorns, bees and wildflowers. We trampled the mounds of earth left all over the garden by the subterranean intruders who'd taken up residency. I walked over a huge deposit of hundreds, thousands of worms. I jumped on them and squished them with my baby kangaroo. I hurt my ankles, and as I hopped towards the thick greenery I had to keep ducking to pick ticks off my skin or brush away nettles, bobbing up and down in a funny monkey-like way. When we reached the woods, I untied my baby and let him walk around on the downhill slope. A moment later, I lost sight of him. I began to run, arms flailing. Words came out of my mouth. I heard a gunshot and turned my head furtively, ingenuously, like a faun. I pricked up my ears. What was that loud noise? Where was the baby? My heart was beating so fast I thought I'd see him covered in mud among the fallen leaves. Then I started to look for him as only a mother can look for her child. Not by running or walking, not through physical actions at all. I found him lying on some branches higher up than even I would have climbed. Cu-cu ma-ma. He motioned to me with his hand. He'd only just started walking and already he was climbing trees. I've given birth to a little savage. I scrambled up to where he was and we sat holding on to each other. From there we saw the water sweep across the woods, which were more like a jungle by now. We saw the little rabbit skulls. And the death of a tiny chick that had got separated from its nest. Its mother's sharp black beak, wide open in fear. I gave the baby swamp water from the pond to taste. Petals from the most colourful and fragrant flowers to eat. Leaves to chew on for their sap. We mimicked the calls of the animals around us, becoming part of them. The diurnal and nocturnal birds answered us, and we heard the cry that begins peacefully and turns mournful halfway through. The pleasant vowel Aa that changes into the hoarse, fearsome consonant Och. The bird that calls out and becomes two birds: sane and insane, tame and murderous. I dunked my son in the icy water and baptised him by mistake. May God forgive me. He seemed too pale to be real. He wasn't a child but a painting, the sketch of a child, the archetype. He'd begun to fade. Like those beasts that give birth to dead offspring on their way somewhere and spend days kicking at the stillborn creature, attempting to revive it, I shook my child and wrapped him up in my red flesh. He came to at midnight. The hours of the dog and the wolf are over, and it's the bats' turn to take the night. I push at him with my legs, rallying him, but his breathing is still laboured. The road surrounds us, and beyond it the electric fence enclosing the white cows with short horns. We're on hunting ground. Voices are saying our names, but we forgot them long ago. They're looking for us. Blah blah blah or cock a doodle doo, it doesn't matter. They'd be better off keeping their mouths shut. The animals are mocking them. The stag stops in his tracks, embalmed, eyes of glass. He's so touchingly still. He's the man of my life, the one who can see into my infinite sadness. The others are just men. What good are men when they speak a language that falls short? My real man isn't human, I know, but who wants to be human? My son pulls on the stag's triangular ear and its black snout, but the animal doesn't laugh. Let's camouflage ourselves, let's cover our skin with dirt and greenery. They're shouting louder now. It's the neighbours with giant lanterns, here to pull us out of our wilderness. It's Daddy. Half the world's out there but none of them does us any good. The crowd is like a stabbing pain. It can only do harm.

The phone rang. I left the baby with his nappy hanging loose and managed to say a few words. Hello, mmm, that's right, yes. But my tone gave me away. I could have said, How's the family? Or, Did you hear there's a huge storm coming our way? But there's no getting around the tone of my voice, and the way I have of fixing my gaze on something, of rudely narrowing my eyes. My tongue dry or too wet. I heard a shout. They're killing my son. Or they've caught a calf by the neck. Something's going on. An organised slaughter out there. But no, it's in here. My husband comes towards me and I think this time he'll finally touch me. I swallow, but nothing goes down. He's taken everything. He's left me with half a mouth, ragged and full of rasping air. My better half had been listening in from behind the door – yes, the playwright of my life is that mediocre. He told me to hang up and leave the baby with his grandmother so we could go out right now and practise driving. He said I needed to get my licence urgently, that I couldn't go on being so useless, that what if there was an emergency and I had to get somewhere in a hurry. He said that out in the countryside there's not as much room for people to be fools. I have the feeling that as soon as I get into the car he'll strangle me with the steering wheel. You're ruining the clutch, put it in first gear, get the gear right, he yells. It was that moment in the evening when flies finally stop buzzing around horses' eyes, after torturing the animals every time they blink, all day long. They take off in black spools, dark swirls, leaving the horses blind and alone. The animals were following us curiously. And as my family gradually succumbs to the radiation of infidelity, I stick my hand through the barbed wire that separates beasts from men and hope the horse will gallop with its jaw hanging open and release its desire. Even as I hear the words divorce and papers, I think how wonderful it is to be stretched out on a filthy scrap of ground with a municipal cemetery nearby. Surrounded by dung and straw but with a ravenous body on top of me, a body that's neither a corpse nor a prisoner of war. Such delicious luxury to have the weight of a man pressing on my guts, his feet and head level with my own. A peasant walks by with a gun on his shoulder, a twisted tree offends him somehow and he shoots at it to kill. Tatatatata. He would have liked to fight in a real battle. The trunk is riddled with holes, but it doesn't fall. The tree staggers but keeps its footing. My husband pretends he's not crying. The man on top of me moves in waves, taking me by the neck, sinking me deeper. I don't understand the hidden workings of passion, but it carries me away nonetheless. The curtain drops. Lawyers and the dissolution of the family by mutual consent. Numbers, signatures, laws, paperwork. But that's not going to happen. I want someone who'll leave me shaken like the sight of a dying animal. When I'm overcome with lust, I'm a cow with a trapped head. If I burn with desire, I'm a stag walking into a wood the way a bridegroom walks into a church.

I remember what's not here. An island of men who are searching for beauty and find it only in the vastness of confinement. I admit I'm sadistic. I'm always saying that nothing is possible without the soul, just as no image is possible without its other. But I have no other. I have no soul. A young lover once promised to write the fatal sign on my womb and take me away with him to fertile lands. What became of him? That night is a hundred thousand nights ago and that lover is lost. I'm still waiting for him to appear among the smoky spirals that emerge from my mouth. I've had a series of smells burnt into me: a pair of hands in the twilight, the soft skin of somebody's back, a bewitched throat. Then it was over, and they were all gone. I'm still a witch who's waiting to cast spells. Our neighbour died of a heroin overdose with his baby in his arms. The woman in the house with the boarded-up windows suffocated on the smoke of her own fire. The animals die out before reproducing. That's what death looks like in these parts. Whereas my sun-soaked nights on the island were filled with stimulating chats, daydreams, furious kisses. Whereas in those golden years of my life, everything was an ecstasy of sexual reawakening. A wave of antipathy to the world wells up from deep within me. I don't know what these animals are up to. They're forming a circle around me and watching me, dumbfounded, their jaws practically unhinged from their bodies. I fall to my knees before them. If a local were to pass by now, basket in hand, gathering mushrooms and berries, they'd think this was some kind of pagan ritual.

Now I'm the one doing the spying. On my bicycle.

Husband on the road, or so he says, and child safe at his grandmother's. I bet she's feeding him up, making the most of having someone else around. Inside his house, the father's trying to calm the spasms of his empty-headed angel, his little fish with no scales. I see him swaying from side to side, gripping her bones. Crushing her hips. Her eyes rolling with wild delight at her father. What's the father doing to his daughter? The girl complains, dribbles on his face. A little she-wolf, caged and spoilt. The father squeezes her too hard. He pinches her skin, smothers her with kisses. The left side of her brain is flat, she takes after her mother. She can't talk, can't walk, can't sit up. She doesn't cry. She doesn't drink water and doesn't focus her gaze, can't even pretend to. The convulsions subside. The electricity leaves her body and she goes limp. The daughter lies exhausted in her crib, her legs and curls protruding through the bars. Her textureless brain won't stop her body in its path towards putrefaction, or from menstruating or ceasing to menstruate. I see him wrap her in a feather duvet, turning her into a pheasant with a ring of white plumage around her neck. What could she be thinking? Will she remember this when she's old enough to have a memory? What will she say to herself without words, without language? What's going on in her failing mind? A child in a state of senility. The father lulls her to sleep, he strokes her ankles. I want him so badly I could put my fist through the window, climb in and rape him right then and there, with the infant breathing softly nearby and the tiny glow-in-the-dark stars twinkling on the ceiling. My desire shuts its eyes and summons him to me, and my clever brain skilled in rhetorical trickery folds flat. He looks out at the night as if it were a chest sunk deep in the mysteries of the ocean and I hide in the vegetation like a mouse under the furniture. He comes out in slippers with his belt undone, and grabs an iron rod as a precaution before coming to see what's moving in the bushes. He's a bow-legged caveman with his hair hanging loose. A primate. I back away and fall into a ditch. The mud obliterates my femininity. He aims at my legs. He wants to take the intruder's head off to make him feel like a man. A family man. He wants to shout about it from the mouth of the cave. He prods my gut and the iron rod sinks into my flabby flesh. He smells his armpits to work up the courage. Lying in the pit, all I want is to take off my skirt in a bedroom with a view of the river, or one where I can hear the river rushing towards me, sharp stones and all. I want to have my legs on top of those of the tall, bony father; to take off my skirt and press my knickers into his face, my hips onto his eyebrows. Make him even more cross-eyed. Make his mouth fuchsia. His iron rod feels its way along my neck. No animals roam the pastoral horizon; they've all been dragged away by the current. The air is filled with fine ash. He pokes me again and I shake violently. Finally, he recognises my movements and rescues me, pulling me up by my muddy rump. Through the window we hear his little girl howl. 'Lord, give us the peace that the earth cannot give.' And from there, in his arms, I heard the bwa bwa bwa or pfa pfa pfa of water against a coast that was sometimes rocky, sometimes made of concrete, and sometimes a gentle slope slipping down towards the shore. It's time for dinner, for the monastery, for ruin. He takes me by the hand and leads me towards his house, but I go into the attic alone. I have no idea where his wife is. A single bed, a chair, a sentimental wall-hanging embroidered by the other woman. No need for extra furnishings. He comes in and locks the door behind him with an iron key. From downstairs, the mother and daughter will think we're two rodents dancing tip tap tip tap tip tap. His presence makes me light-headed. He takes me by the neck and inhales me. I let go of my body. Let it burn, let it turn red. He takes off his clothes and lies his six-foot-two frame down on top of me. His feet hang off the mattress. We mangle each other and I see myself reflected as though in a kaleidoscope. My open mouth is many mouths. In one feline motion, I turn over and climb on top of him. I'd have sodomised him if I could. A sodomising rodent. I'm close, forgetting where I am, who I am. There's no day or night, no attic or countryside. But first, I look at his face and do everything I can to retain it. And obviously I can't, and the dark light of the morning after comes flooding in to find us lying one inside the other.

And just like that he got up from the narrow bed in the middle of the night while I was lying there naked. He'd left me a prosaic note. And so the terror began. A few hours earlier we'd been levitating, but what does the night before matter by the morning after? I leapt out of the little bed, my mouth pasty. There was no one downstairs; the three of them had gone shopping. How many times had he moved in and out of me, the attic air turning to honey around us. How many times had desire brushed against the unbearable, the mouth of an alligator open as wide as it could go. The river pulled me along and I was nothing but a dry branch. I pedalled the twelve miles back home wanting to vomit. I pedalled and pedalled without separating myself from the taste of him in my saliva. Desire – sticky, putrid, servile desire – followed me all the way down the road. I'll need aggressive laser treatment to help me forget his jaw and rid myself of his forehead. Far away, among the plastic-wrapped hay bales, a boy I'd never seen was doing a wheelie on his scooter, a cigarette clinging to his lower lip. My son in a few years, perhaps. I keep pedalling with my long legs, wishing I could stomp on the ground like a mare with fangs.

It's been five weeks now and I can't figure out if this means anything to you. Stop counting, will you? It's horrible. Five weeks, thirty-five days, eight hundred and forty hours. I can't stop counting. You'll have to because I can't go on like this. And it's not five, it's three, or have you forgotten that time on the way back from our holiday? It's five! It was the night you got back after you'd been away, remember? The day we watched the final episode of the show about those guys stuck on an island. I wouldn't leave you alone, and after we argued we did it on the sofa. We put a towel down first. I remember the position and everything. When we'd finished we watched the rest of the show and ate chips. I think we did it again after that, or are you saying we didn't do it while we were away? Whatever, I don't want to argue. No, I'd remember if we had. What, are you keeping track of every time? I don't need to. Fine, moving on, do you want to now? Sure, tonight if you like, but don't say yes just to do me a favour. Do you think I've ever done it as a favour? Do you think I've forgotten how beautiful you are? Right, before or after dinner? After would be better. Around twelve? Sure, twelve's good, after we put him to bed, but I'm telling you, don't do it as a favour. Okay, let's watch the news first, apparently they've been launching more missiles or something. But were those missiles or the beating of my heart? Throwing him off balance isn't hard, but if I can make him laugh, I've got thirty seconds to do whatever I want with him. Do you think your low libido is because of the cigarettes? What low libido? Annoying him is the easiest thing of all. That's what smoking does, it lowers your sex drive. Don't be silly, smoking doesn't affect me at all. So how come you never feel like doing it? Feel like doing what? But after his post-dinner cigarette, the smell of the food piled up in the sink, and the coffee, I went to look for him, one of my shoulders bare. He said he was exhausted. I'm *sausted*, I heard, like a gargle through his mouthful of smoke. His lips and gums were so thick with tar that I held my breath to avoid getting a waft of his. I lingered a bit. I'd waxed, showered and put new knickers on. I stuck around to see if he'd grab me by the waist, if there'd be foreplay, if he felt like throwing me against a wall or onto the sofa like the last time, five weeks ago, not three. If it were three it wouldn't be so bad, and besides, holidays don't count. So nothing. Nothing at all. And this really gets me riled up, it sharpens my teeth into blades. I swear at him, give him the finger, grow hooves. I go into the bathroom, close the door and throw myself down onto the cold tiles. I stick my feet in the shower, make spastic movements. But there's no audience. My husband needs to take a dump. I don't open the door. This is my small revenge, let him hold it in. I hold it in too: I'm a snake in heat coiled up between the bidet and the toilet. Open the door, please, we'll do it after, I promise. He's bribing me, but screw him. I'm begging you, it's not funny. And then, having climbed onto the toilet, I deliver a lengthy existential monologue, adding some philosophical and psychoanalytic touches for good measure. When I'm done, he says: It's all in your head. That's all he ever says. In the end I feel sorry for him and leave the bathroom. He gives me an insipid kiss that does nothing for me. I need a buffalo and all I get is a porcupine. He shoves me away from the bathroom door. I hear him defecate, the sound of his shit dropping into the water. I wait for him in bed, try to read something, but all I can think about is satiating my body: it's chasing after me, sweating. I toss the book aside. The baby is all twisted up in his sleep, coughing like a worker in a Cuban tobacco factory. I straighten him out and decide to go to sleep. My husband is still in the bathroom, playing on his phone. I end up taking off my bra, the underwire hurts, and changing out of my knickers. I scrub my face clean and slather on some lotion. Afterwards, nothing. At dawn, I'm woken by a shrill, trumpet-like scream. A strange whistling sound. The fire in the living room has gone out. I blow on it but that just sends ash flying everywhere, including up my nose. I spit. I sneeze. I have an allergic reaction. Nasal blood. I try to light the fire. The uproar continues outside. Men and animals are fighting it out. A chicken truck has crashed into a car carrying an average family, two point four children in a pile-up. Or it's a kangaroo giving birth to a troop of joeys and they've got stuck on the way out. I leave the house barefoot. I get soaked, slip on the stones, look for the source of the tumult of voices and growls. I walk down the road, through the woods and to the stretch of wasteland scattered with used condoms where the tourists go to procreate. It's coming from the sky. Hundreds of birds are criss-crossing each other, confused. No one's leading them. North and south are mixed up. The baby is crying his quota of morning torment. He's had his nightmare about a hungry wolf climbing in through the window. There's no smoke detector in his room. I put him to bed with my husband. I wrap their arms around each other and they lie there, sound asleep, breathing the air from each other's mouths. My vampiric offspring is going to end up a smoker. I go back outside. For the first time, I feel drawn to the sky. The birds are raising the feathers on their wings, they're riled up like bulls. Then one of them heads south and the rest follow, screeching off into the distance. Back in the house I find the baby under our bed, screaming at the top of his lungs like another bird. I don't know what we're doing with our tiny deformity, with our flesh. What we're doing with our conjoined entrails. We're letting him grow up among shrubs and bones. We're letting him get scraped and knocked about. How could you leave him there when you can see I'm sleeping, he said. Are you out of your mind? Then he drifted off again. I lay down between my husband and my son and watched them inhale and exhale as they abandoned themselves to the heavy breathing of sleep. I looked at one face and then at the other, and then at myself in the middle. I eventually got bored of their features and was alarmed to find that, after staring at them for so long, I no longer recognised them.

The baby woke up at seven on the dot, not caring in the slightest that it was Sunday. His body clock never fails. The fields were covered in fog. I might have been at the beach or in the desert for all I knew. It could have been me spacing out or delirium tremens, but no, it was stinking reality. Winter was almost here, and all you could see was wood piled high in every porch. I'll spend the rest of the day watching the way the ash floats through the air. I devoted the morning to swearing at the baby. I said all kinds of nasty things to him. To the baby. There's nothing I didn't say, it was one insult after another. My son's got a foul mouth for a mother. I filled him up with dirty words, the poor thing. I hope he doesn't recognise any of them, that he doesn't go around saying fucking hell in front of everyone after this. He looked at me and said, Mum, pee, and I told him to go and pee on his own, and to feed himself while he was at it. That wintery Sunday hadn't got off to a good start. Things were going from bad to worse and it wasn't even two o'clock. I'm fed up with the fact that it's not okay to bad-mouth your own baby or walk around firing a gun. We spent the day in a stupor thanks to the gas leaking from the pipes. There must be a leak, a broken pipe, otherwise where's this rotten smell coming from, a neighbour said once, her dress unbuttoned. I'm sure that's why my husband's still snoozing, it's been almost a day now. Every so often a long-distance lorry passes by. My baby and I go out into the garden wrapped in lambswool jumpers and he says vroom, vroom, while I gasp for air. The fire inside still burns.

We were only just waking up from the weekend and already we were fighting. At half past eight I let out the first scream, at nine-twenty I threatened to leave, and at nine-fifty I said I'd make his life a living hell. By ten past ten, I was standing like a ram in the middle of the road with my straw hat on, suitcase in hand and flies in my eardrums. Bikes, lorries, lame dogs: they're forever dodging me, brushing past me, missing me by an inch. The neighbours in their cars are forever beeping their horns at me and swearing. Move over, get out of the way. They're all afraid of spending the night at the police station defending their actions. No one wants to pay for a lawyer or deal with legal issues, so they avoid the bureaucracy of the justice system. Anyone in a blue uniform is the devil. Me getting run over on the side of the road is the least of their worries. Me winding up covered in brown blood, my twisted body sprawled out on the ground between the septic tank and the chicken coop. Or flying through the air and shattering against the corrugated metal of a garage door. At most they'd sympathise a bit, but not with me. With the little boy who's now motherless. That's what people say at the wakes of young addicts, as they help themselves to more coffee. Poor thing, left without a mother. Poor little orphan. No one grieves for the wretched woman with scarred arms who was consumed by the misery of life. Everyone fusses over the little boy who's crawling around on all fours near the coffin. They give him biscuits and he's a monkey. And here I am in this bitter autumn-winter, still standing in the middle of the road. I don't know why I remain here, like an insect with its antennae raised, a scarecrow, the same suitcase I arrived with full of clothes and books. I like to walk barefoot on the tarmac. I like it when my feet turn grey. My husband dismantles the plastic pool and pours the rusty water onto the grass. Thousands of ants drown but no one cares. I'm waiting for a call. The murmur of the main road is mental noise; the cars that shoot by like arrows are my ideas. I'm waiting for a call and I confuse the distant sounds coming off the main road with my vibrating phone. I hear a meow and answer hello, the blow of a hammer and I grab the phone. Everything is one big distortion. My son's toy car, vroom vroom, could suddenly run me over. The guy up the ladder in low-slung trousers turns on a chainsaw that shrieks when it climaxes. My mobile phone was burning my hand all day long and he never called. I come and go along the road, the pebbles between my toes, while my baby's forehead is blazing. The motorcycle doesn't pass by either. Desiring someone is like having a boiled sweet stuck to your neck, your scalp, your jugular. My husband comes looking for me when it's too late to see. Not even the most brightly coloured fruit or the red stop signs are visible. My husband comes along, whistling a tune of victory. He gestures at me and his hands are bursts of silver, it looks like he's signalling a plane for landing. At least bring the buggy in, he shouts. And from the tips of my toes to the top of my head, I'm a shadow. Okay, fine, I'm coming. Let's have some dinner, watch TV and go to bed. Flames burn in the twisted fireplace. The warmth of the hearth but my eyes set fire to everything. I stay in the road a little while longer. Intoxicated, repugnant, harassed. My son points to a rooster and says cock-a-doo-dle-doo. We're getting worse and worse at speaking. I see zombie spiders marching along in single file. It's his fingers, they're stroking my face. Desire is to blame, this destructive hunger. The words come out of nowhere: Did you check his temperature today? I can't recall. His temperature is rising. It's pushing forty. Mine is too, but who cares about the mother's health. They come first. I should call an ambulance, but I don't move, I can't take so much as a step. I'm still by the roadside, inches from the passing cars that don't see me. The wind rocks the grass from side to side, rippling it, separating it from the earth. I look at nature and she looks at me. Desire is an alarm I can't turn off. My baby chews his dummy to pieces, om nom nom. My baby wants to be an adult. He puts his shoes on and runs away. It would do him good. To start from scratch. My little one whacks me on the lower lip, saying, No, Mummy! Mummy, no! I raise my finger and with the gesture of a doting mother, say: Don't do that, okay? He laughs in my face. Are you coming? I'm coming, says my voice from the blue country night. And then the three of us are in an ambulance, and later, at the end of the night, we all return home with our arms around each other. Antibiotics and cold compresses. Not even digging a hole, a pit, would be enough. It needs to be thrown into the desert and devoured by wild beasts. Desire, that is.

I wanted it all to be over quickly, or to happen in legitimate self-defence. It's not that I was seriously considering killing him, but at that moment, in that light, I was tempted. And on top of everything else the dog wouldn't stop barking. It barked and barked and barked. The stupid thing even barks at the wheels of parked tractors. Someone please slit its vocal cords once and for all. A quick death and then on to something else. It's not that I was going to kill him under that moon, but everything's a matter of seconds. And those seconds were... how can I put it. During those seconds, I felt comfortable with danger. A sort of erotic communion with a spade that was lying around, with a rake, with the blade of the rusty knife that hung from my husband's *gaucho* trousers, swinging like a bell. Just to be clear, I'm not a killer, not even close. I don't fit the profile, nor do I have some sob-story that would help me get off scot-free with a *she acted in a state of high emotion.* I wasn't raped by my grandfather or my uncle. I did have a childhood, though I've forgotten it now. I don't remember anything before yesterday, when I fled the scene. The experts are going to have their work cut out for them with my case. I'm the product of a normal family, too normal. The prosecutor rubs his hands. A normal family is the most sinister kind. Bullshit. Or there's nothing more sinister than being the product of a normal family. These demons are all mine. I raised them, fed them, fattened them up. You'll eventually marry him and have three kids, because one child leads to another, like lighting one cigarette on the end of the last. You'll buy this house or a bigger one you find online, one with a real pool and a security barrier hooked up to an alarm in case a child falls in. That's what I think. Give me a second here. While he's strutting around behind me, I ask: If I fall to my knees and hurt myself, if I break a bone, if I learn to pray, is there a chance I can turn back time, turn it back to nowhere even, or will this story simply end with the mother who forgot to set the alarm? And it was then, after that thought, which I'd say was realistic, insightful even, rather than dark, that I reached the highest state of lucidity and felt around for the gun. Lucidity needs to be treated with extreme caution. Those moments when the mind, no matter how poorly it functions, sees clearly. I'm not laughing at him, but he's just ridiculous behind me, his pelvis jutting out, while my eyes focus on the green tarp the neighbour uses to cover his pile of crap. It's unbelievable how much stuff people hoard out here in the country. The more space they have, the more shit they cram into it. Crates, shelves, sheds overflowing with knick-knacks. We should really have a bonfire. It's not that I'm assuming I want to slit his throat. I'm only saying that submission pisses me off. The dog keeps barking. Who knows who it's barking at now. My body is dry. Dried up. Dried out. Must be the cold. I walked away, not knowing if I was stepping on its head or some manure. Just as well everything was over quickly. Very quickly.

She woke up to the sight of her husband sitting in a striped deckchair reading the paper. She listened as he turned the pages, saw which article he was reading and in which section. She heard him clear his throat, saw him uncross his legs. When will I start feeling like he's dead? When will I be able to pray for him? These are tricky questions to answer at four in the morning, Mum. Why don't you take something so we can go back to sleep? And he huffed and puffed with impatience. My mother-in-law's bed shows signs of her battle with sleep. You go ahead, go back to bed. But for her it was impossible. Her eyelids were leaden. What does it mean for a man to die? she said from the heights of her aged lust. You're asking me? I said, sunken into my pyjamas. The framed pictures, the prayer cards, the photographs. The piles of clothing, the towels, the perfume. And the toothbrush, the comb, the socks. His ointment, his talcum powder, his underlined books. And his armchair and his pipe and matches. And his underwear, vests and shaving cream. And most of all, none of this. The way he breathes, the mark his behind leaves on the cushion, his morning breath, the goat noises he makes when he chews, when he stretches and cracks his knuckles while talking to you. His still body in a chair or standing up. Or leaning against the wall. And so much more than all of this. An intangible, inscrutable way of looking at things, at a blowfly, a baby caterpillar, a stretch of barren land. An unfulfilled desire that's ferocious enough to set an entire village on fire. The figure of a man in the road. From afar we can't quite make out what it is. A head. A skull to put on the mantelpiece. My mother-in-law asks question after question. What am I supposed to do, son, stare at the sky? Drink your tea, Mum, go on. The son worries about her health. Parents become children when they're in pain. I'm still curled up on the sofa by the fire that's gone out. I look at myself in my slippers… I want to be Heidi. I understand my mother-in-law so well that I want to run over and climb into her chest. Stick my fingers into her eyes. I understand her so well that I want to get inside her dressing gown. We could have four hands, maybe that would comfort her. I don't say anything. I play the role of daughter-in-law, but really I'm a wolf in sheep's clothing. Dazed, I stare at the cupboard full of jars of jam made by the man who was buried, summer '94, summer '97, autumn 2002, each with its label. Understanding one another is too violent. It's better to keep quiet, play dumb. That's what I do. My husband stirs his mother's herbal tea, refusing to put sugar in it, and while he rubs her shoulders he says, There's nothing you can do, Mum. Dad's not here any more. There are no words, nothing I can say will bring him back. Let him rest in peace, he tells her. Pffft, boring. I can't stand the things people say about the dead. He doesn't know how to stop the bullet that will reach her sooner or later. He thinks that by doing things for her he's actually helping. The guillotine's blade has been raised, but no one can see it's about to fall. Mother and son hug each other, but the mother is no longer there. This balloon moving in the breeze is unstoppable, this airy thing that wafts across the vacant sky and is snatched away by a gust of wind. Shrugging my shoulders, I look at her without thinking, the way you look at a person who's ill, a person who's fading away while the rest of us remain on our feet sneaking glances at our watches. I wish she hadn't stopped cooking for me, filling the house with delicious smells and bringing bread and butter to her offspring. What does it mean for a man to die? What became, what didn't become, of his life? It's six in the morning, dear. Let it go. Then we stopped answering her questions. There was simply no point.

When I'm almost at the slope that drops down into the woods, I hear a woman discussing *Mrs Dalloway* on the radio. The programme's already begun, but I still know they're talking about her. How far are you planning to go? My husband gets out of the moving car, pulling the handbrake so I don't end up in the lake. You did well today, he says, your driving's getting better and better, you just need to learn how to control the car around curves and how to reverse. I see him walk off to bang nails into the new terrace. I stay in the car, the windows foggy. I turn up the volume and take my foot off the clutch. '*Mrs Dalloway* is a novel about time and the interconnectivity of human existence.' How long has it been since I've heard that kind of language? Interconnectivity. Fucking hell. I try to turn the plastic cog but the seat won't recline. My husband watches me swear from afar, reading my lips and smiling. He has a cigarette behind his ear like a shopkeeper. I wonder what I'd make of this very woodland, this rustic setting, the half-built house, the man nailing down planks of wood, if a critic said my writing dealt with 'the interconnectivity of human existence'. I burst out laughing. It's nervous laughter. The other day I was trying to read something when I heard little footsteps going tap tap tap and saw a mouse calmly making its way under my bookshelf. I had to call the neighbour, who came by armed with a stick. Then they brought over a grey cat they'd found wandering around by the sewers and let it loose in my bedroom. It sniffed the whole place and covered my bed in fur, but didn't do a thing. So these days I read surrounded by mouse traps.

They're talking about Septimus, the traumatised war hero character who also battles manic depression and madness, and who really does throw himself out of the window. I think about the palliative effects that writing, or throwing myself out the window, could have on my life. Those who write don't need leather jackets because in their universe it's always summer. I grab the handbrake. On nights like this, I find it comforting to know that when I get home late with my tongue all furry there won't be any snakes coming out of the taps. And that there never will be, because it's impossible. A tiger in the living room, though. That could happen. The thought of someone discussing a character I've created the way they do Mrs Dalloway. I turn off the radio and try to hear the birds talking in Greek, though what a poisoned inheritance that would be. And what would it be like, really, what would it be like, I repeat to myself, kicking the steering wheel. Fucking hell. And then I fell asleep in there, the seat half-reclined, my legs making marks on the glass. Much later I opened one eye and saw a blackbird with a bright yellow beak hopping towards me.

I've been needing the loo since lunch but it's impossible to do anything other than be a mother. Enough already with the crying. He cries and cries and cries. I'm going to lose my mind. I'm a mother, full stop. And I regret it, but I can't even say that. Who would I say it to? To the boy sitting on my lap, sticking his hand in my plate of cold leftovers, playing with a chicken bone? No! Leave that alone, you'll choke. I chuck him a biscuit. He gives it back. My mouth is full of his saliva, of crumbs. My arm has a piece of tomato stuck to it. I put another biscuit in his mouth before he's finished this one and he chokes. I take no responsibility for anything he might think of me. I brought him into this world, and that's plenty. I'm a mother on autopilot. He's whining now and it's worse than his crying. I lift him up and give him a fake smile, clenching my teeth. Mummy was happy before the baby came. Now Mummy gets up each day wanting to run away from the baby while he just cries harder and harder. I need the loo, but his interminable clucking and grousing makes it impossible. What does he want from me. What do you want? He doesn't let me leave him. He arches his back. Yesterday I had to take him with me to the loo, but today I'd rather shit myself. I call my husband. I need reinforcements. While I'm dialling, the baby hangs off one of my shoulders. He's going to tear me apart. He sticks something viscous to my bellybutton. Please pick up, please pick up. Hello, listen love, I need you to come home now, I can't go on like this. No, you can't be a little while, you need to come now, you don't understand, you don't even want to understand, I won't last till tonight. I hang up because he's pretending not to understand. Maybe he'll get worried and come home at once. We linger near the phone, tangled up in the cable, just in case he calls back. I carry the baby to the door to see if there's anyone passing by that I can give him to. But we don't have the sort of neighbours I need. All we have are bastards. What if I knock on the door of the elderly woman with the barred-up windows and aggressive pet turtles? I'm sure he could entertain her. It'd be like having a television, like going to the cinema. No one goes past, no one wants him. Nothing moves and the air is still, possessed. I leave him lying at my feet. He twists, stretches, screams at me, takes off his nappy and unbuttons my shoes, chews on the leather straps. I look at him the way a crab looks at a child. A racing car carrying a family drives by. Their heads are sticking out of the windows. It's nighttime and I'm still leaning against the gate. I see myself when I was pregnant, thinking I was carrying a gargoyle inside me. I see myself giving birth, expelling him. We're getting bitten, I should go inside, get the fire going and clear away the lunch plates full of red ants loading up on food for the winter. The father didn't come home. I load the sweaty, hungry, sharp-nailed baby onto my back and take him inside. I should probably make him some pasta or soup, pull up some vegetable or other from the neighbour's garden, but I can't be bothered. Being a mother is so very unexciting. I can hardly keep it in. Then I feel this pain inside me. I drop him and cross my legs. I run off to shut myself away. He wails hysterically as though mourning the loss of a loved one at a Chinese funeral. I can't cope with it and let him in. I think about how disgusting it all is.

You're never cool, you're never zen. The same words the entire journey. You're never cool, you're never zen. I'm a mess. I cross and uncross my legs, and don't even get me started on what my chest is doing. My son's in the back in his car seat. Out of the window, tiny town after tiny town and the hill showing off a landscape that could be beautiful. Act normal, calm down, he says, and gets out to go to the bakery. I get out too, cross the road and then look back at the car. The son doesn't take his eyes off the father, who's buying pastries, selecting them from behind the glass. What kind of chocolate is that one made of? Are there any with cream? How many should I get, love? The baker, her eyes drooping down around her nose, waits with tongs in hand. Her fingers are covered in icing sugar. A quick look inside, and I turn and head back to the rubbish. No idea what I said. I pace up and down the street. My husband comes out with a cardboard container that he puts on my lap. Careful with the box. I bought six. Three and three. Two of each. I keep hold of the door handle. Trembling. Burning. In a garden I see a threesome of animals, one at the back and another smelling the arse of the one in front. Which gets rid of what little appetite I had. My stomach churns; imagine having sex in this cold. The car takes a curve in the road. I drop the box. There's cream all over the seat. Shouts. I do what I can to save the pastries, to put each back in its place. My husband looks at them with contempt and says: They have your finger marks all over them. I try to fix this and only make it worse. You're never relaxed, he tells me. I never see you cool and calm. You ruin everything. And he lights a cigarette in the car, something that's not allowed in our family. And I don't say anything because whatever. What kind of a family is this anyway? And the window's open, the cold breeze going straight for the baby's throat – the baby who's still on antibiotics. But what can you do. All three of us are coughing by the time we reach our friends' house. A thick beige carpet, a little door that opens onto the autumn leaves, the children's rusty bikes and a few spare tyres. A tent set up in the middle of the living room, a white dog licking the children's mouths. A teapot, more boxes of pastries, napkins, teaspoons, gossiping guests. Isn't it lovely here. Where other people live. I'm amazed at the sight of so many civilised people. Their hair's combed, they smell nice. Hi, how's it going, hey, it's been forever, how's everything with you, all good thanks, and how about you? Hugs, pats on the back. More patting. More hugging. Everyone around the table saying happy new year, though that was a while ago now. There's a mirror in front of us. No one looks like they're in pain, no one's gone mad, no one's summoning the dead. Streamers from the last time one of the kids had a birthday party. Titi, don't put that in your mouth, get out of there! No! The stairs! It's snack time, kids! Who wants some milk? Time for food, children! And how about you guys, what do you give him? My husband and I look at each other for the first time. What do we give him? Anything. Whatever the other children are having. I didn't bring his snack. I forgot it. I brought the nappy cream, the changing mat, an extra pair of pants, the drops. The children eat their snacks together and the house looks like a kindergarten. My baby laughs, I don't recognise his laughter. They go out onto the patio, climb things, roll around in the leaves. We grown-ups help ourselves to little platefuls of food. My husband is too embarrassed to open the box of pastries we brought and leaves it off to one side. No one touches it. The six pastries melt. The afternoon wears on and it's a lumbering animal, a giant seal entering the water. Behind us are the vineyards, the stakes stuck in the earth. Someone asks what's in the box. No one notices my fingerprints. Children crying, children hitting each other. The parents look up to see if the crying child is theirs so they can go to the rescue. My husband is eating a piece of sponge cake and suddenly feels sick. A stabbing pain in his ribs. Everyone stares at him and eventually someone says: Call a doctor! and they go out to look for one among the donkeys and wineries. Ah, doctors. I watch the scene from my chair. They don't call me over, they don't involve me, they don't consider me up to the task. A doctor, they shout, a doctor! The rest of us are a useless bunch. They go from house to house, coming across all sorts of people, but a doctor is hard to find. You've got to study to be a doctor. They finally come back with a vet who'd been helping a cow give birth, his arms and hands covered in amniotic fluid. They lie my husband down on the carpet. The vet, who's used to treating animals and not humans, puts on latex gloves. The kids form a circle around the two of them, hoping something will appear, thinking it's a magic trick. I do too, I think I'm about to witness a birth. I don't want the scene to end, don't want to go back home. See you soon, take care, my regards to the family. See you later, see you, see you soon. My husband says to me: My heart almost stopped. Is that my fault? I ask. It's a warning sign. And what do you want me to do about the warning sign? I want you to pay attention to it. Okay, okay, I say. I want to take my shoe off and throw it at him. No one tried any of our pastries, he says. I bought them only to throw them away. I want to take off down the street, limping. Someone did have some actually, I thought, but there's no point in arguing. You don't respect me, the box is just one example.

Do you deserve my respect? There's no point in arguing. He went on to say something about the box representing marriage, the family, and how I dropped it, how I try to fix things but it's always too late. I'm barely listening. I don't understand his metaphors. It must be that I don't have the brains for them. My mind is somewhere else, like I've been startled awake by a nightmare. I want to drive down the road and not stop when I reach the irrigation ditch. I want to run over the flowers in a yellow race against myself. What's up with you? he says. I look as though I were a daughter with no parents. Can't you raise him on your own? I ask. If so I'll jump out of the car this very minute. The baby was in the back, smiling and showing off his three teeth. I'll jump out now and next time your pastries will be fine. The fields flew at me, full of zigzagging bullets and military planes soaring upside down. I'll jump, I shout, I'll jump, and I open the door and stick out a leg. When we get home, he asks: What should we have for dinner? I put the apron on and chop onion after onion after onion into thin slices until I cut my finger open. And I laugh. The more serious things are, the more I want to laugh. I throw myself down onto the mud-splattered floor. The whole pastry ordeal strikes me as hilarious, for example. Cover your mouth when you cough. Cover your mouth when you sneeze. Cover your mouth when you smoke, I hear myself say. I spend my whole life covering him up. I'm so dirty, so stubborn, so mean that it's scary. The house reeks of onions.

I use my sleeping husband's hand to touch myself. He's not looking at me, he's dreaming. He uses my dead hand to touch himself. I'm not looking at him, I'm asleep. We're in separate bedrooms, on separate mattresses. There's been a mistake. We're not meant to be one. No one wants to be a Siamese twin, to have their organs stuck to someone else's. He smiles while he dreams. I don't make him smile. I swear at him. I punch him, on the shoulder, in the face. He's had it up to here with me and vice versa. We're too much for each other but we carry on. I give him the finger, fuck you, as soon as I get up. Morning, what do you want for breakfast? My outstretched finger in his face. I'd love to break his teeth. The restless child is singing softly between his mum and dad. Who do you love more? asks his Dad, about to explode any second. Is it so difficult for him to say how was your day yesterday? Apparently it is. How was your day yesterday? I ask myself, and answer, fine thanks. I proceed to tell myself about my day, chatting away. I leave the table and he eats my croissant and finishes my coffee. He lets me go, obviously, but then he regrets it and bursts out, You're evil, leading me into the pastures where the vegetation is taller than us. He doesn't give in. He makes me walk blindly, the grasses hitting me in the face like thistles, like the bones of a skeleton. Then he decides to take advantage of the situation and presses himself up against me, but it doesn't go anywhere, and he pushes me further in. I start to speak, I don't know what words come out of my mouth but I keep them coming and he tells me, When you speak it's like the car alarm, it goes on and on, it's unbearable. So I carry on speaking, and now I'm shouting, though I don't know when I raised my voice. Can't you speak without shouting? Can't you give the verbal diarrhoea a rest? He doesn't understand that I can't. Control yourself, he says, I don't understand a thing when you speak non-stop. Why don't you take a pronunciation course? Why don't you do a language exchange with a local? We stop somewhere. Now what? But when I go to say something he snaps at me and walks a few feet away to where I can't see him. I press my fists into my eye sockets. It hurts. What's the point of crying? I'm a startled deer, a sad, sensitive deer. A cool breeze picks up. He doesn't come back to me, but he hasn't left either. I'm just another patch of grass. Nothing happens until suddenly we hear grunts and mooing. I run around in circles and end up on the streaked tarmac. He's there too, watching the show. The cows have been separated from their calves, when just a second ago they were all grazing together quietly, stuffing their faces. These bovine mothers are causing a massive scene, mooing so loudly they grow hoarse, doing everything they can to resist. But their babies get taken away just the same. See you later, calves, I say, waving goodbye. Bon voyage. The cows are still there by the side of the road, stunned. The vultures arrive in time for lunch with their collars of feathers, holding their cutlery and napkins. We go home together, arms around each other. We love each other so much. We sing a catchy little ditty, *why oh why, tell me why could it be, that when a cow's tied up, her calf won't leave.* Someone else's misfortune is a swift kick from a horse.

The wildflowers push through the earth along the side of the road. It gets broken up, forced out. Like us. We'd planned to meet just beyond the parked cars. I look at a walnut tree and think I prefer it to any man. I see a falcon fly over the grass as though it were the sea and think how lucky it is. Then I spot him emerging from the November fog, back where the houses end. He's walking behind a guy pulling on a cart, eeee, eeee, a screeching I feel in my teeth. He seems to be selling fruit and fish. We'd agreed to talk, about how to move forwards, how to stop coming up against a brick wall. But there was no point. To anything. And in the end, he didn't say a word. He might as well have been mute, or have damaged his vocal cords. The fake silence of the road was enough. Kissing on top of speed bumps was enough, or by the side of the road, bathed in toxins from the nuclear power plant. Reaching the summit. That erotic obsession, the word texture giving texture, the colour copper, weeds over our eyes, in our eyes, behind our pupils. We walked along like that, with the babies hanging upside-down, their heads full of blood, swinging to and fro. They drool and we drool too, they shriek like we do. Blinded, we fell into the ditch. We rolled around like two idiots and the babies waved at us from above, reaching out their hands to help us climb back up. And when the night had run its course like a convulsing dog, we said goodbye. And there was a feeling of suffocation riding up my throat, a tick scaling my neck, something winding itself around me, lodging itself inside me, its pincers poking around behind my mouth. I followed the white lines on the road home like a tightrope walker, one foot in front of the other, my bones a step behind like a slave, my arms outstretched. As the sun rose, I pushed the baby along. He was singing softly, la la la. What's he saying? How can he feel like saying anything? My baby wolf with his cold little snout, howling at some planet or other. The house was smoky. There was a note with the dinner menu and a few kisses at the bottom stuck up with Scotch tape. I took off the little wolf's clothing, tugging at his skin. The homeopathic painkiller I swallowed under the covers had no effect whatsoever, and when I woke up a few hours later my skin was violet. That morning I took much longer than usual to do everything. I put on one sock and dropped the other. I did up one button and the other came undone. I brushed my hair and inspected my teeth and nails. Nothing was as it should be. My body wasn't working. It wouldn't allow itself to be dressed, to be tidied. Four hands knocked on the door. What's going on, what's going on. What's going on with what, I say. I take off my sleep costume, my poisonous skin. I recover my sense of smell and my eyelashes, go back to pronouncing words and swallowing. I look at myself in the mirror and see a different person to yesterday. I'm not a mother. On the other side of the door they're whining. Making a fuss. They think it's funny that they're driving me crazy. They lie on the floor and slip dirty messages under the door. 'We love you, Mummy'. They think they're hilarious: the two stooges, painting their lips pink. I try to laugh, to chuckle at the things they say and do. Now the little boy's climbing onto the grown-up's head. They're a monster. I want to celebrate with them but it's impossible. They get impatient: Come out already. Come on, Mummy, come out, says my husband in a high-pitched voice. We're hungry. They won't persuade me. I dress myself as best I can with my sudden club feet and rest a hand on the doorknob. On the other side, silence. Have they gone? Are they waiting for me to open up so they can whack me? I duck down and look through the keyhole. I see shadows, could that be their feet? They're hiding, or they're lying on the floor, or they've run away. I give the door a kick. Now I'm on the other side. Hello? Is anyone out there? Baby, it's Mummy. Are you there? I go out onto the terrace and step on the remains of last night. My husband's having a rough time of it, burning his fingertips on cigarette ends. But desire is a wonderful thing. We have ourselves a dilemma, I say to myself, my fingers grey and covered in cuts. It's not right to run off with another man, said one of the neighbours, and my mother-in-law agreed. It's not right, two drunkards chorused, tossing away their empty bottles. Dance, you wretch. In medieval France, adulterous wives were forced to strip and run around town chasing after a chicken – I hear these words in the distance and don't know why they sound like a message for someone. The stag appears, also in the distance. If only I knew what he was trying to tell me. Then, in a space that's too empty, a pair of figures becomes visible. The sigh of relief that escapes a wolf's mouth. It's my men frolicking, flying, one on top of the other. Even from far away, I can hear the hum of all that happiness.

Every time my husband screws me, I blink and it's like they've felled a tree. Like the blow of an axe. I eat with one hand and the fat drips down my wrist. I talk loudly, drool even, but they screw me anyway. I'm still attractive. Against the wall the way you want it, he says lasciviously. Hands tied as requested. I don't recognise him. It's like he's taken notes. He screws me and my eyes explode again and again. The exorcist. I go blind. A rock to the forehead. He screws me and screws me and it's all destruction, objects fall to the ground and smash. Grandma's porcelain teacups. The little framed pictures we brought back from Italy. My house is a warehouse of glass. My femur hurts. I say nothing. For once, I go with his flow. My tautologically little husband seems to have a new lease of life. The lad's actually woken up. I let myself drown in his fluids. He even calls me whore. He uses that word and his mouth fills up with furious water. Polluted water. These are not his words. Praise the Lord. He's learnt – from having watched the other? But it's no use to me any more. I try to belong to him. I give him my scalp. Take it. I give him my brain. I give him my stretched skin. Tug it. I give him my eyelids, don't care if I lose them. Let my eyes dry out in one blink. I offer myself to him. Take me. Have me. Taste me. I want to be his woman but I look at him with the surprise of a stranger. A woman attacked by a shadow while she's napping. A woman who's groped while she's walking along. I fall over to the side. I feel sick and I'm offered a glass of water. Take a seat, madam, the children say. They offer me salt in the palms of their hands, the way you would a bird. I peck him hard with my beak. It's over. I let him keep touching me. We're covered in saliva. Now comes the hug and the wet kiss. Now comes the hounding of love. I want to fuse into myself. But it's like shooting at your feet, like burying something close to the surface so it sprouts. We're an elderly couple with heatstroke.

But nor is he an idiot. I just look like one, he said. And then one morning at seven-forty, the wind beating about our heads, he said, Come here, sit down. And come here sit down is all you need to hear to know it's over. It's the end. I went weak at the knees. Who cares what comes next. How much time we spend sitting at a table, our arms folded. Whether or not we cry, pack our suitcases, divide our belongings. Who cares about the future, whether there's joint custody, whether the boy is kidnapped by one of his parents, whether we go to trial and there's a lawsuit for child support. Come here sit down and it wasn't even eight in the morning. I had a bitter taste in my mouth after a night that had been rough, tough, bloody. Come here sit down, though later on there's always the consoling thought that things might not be so bad, because wounds heal, because time can be an ally. I felt a stabbing pain in my sex and had to drag myself towards the chair. If I could I'd use a walking stick, dress like an old lady, die my hair grey, take pills for neurological illnesses until my brain made room for them. I want to be an old woman. Unpleasant in every way, repulsive, unbearable. I'd stink. I'd take medication to make it worse, so they'd have to look after me for even longer. And so, with my sex still throbbing, I listened to him, saw him move a mouth that was already very far away, saying words I didn't understand. The leaves broke apart in the air, the scenery shook as if someone was directing us. Then I heard the word treatment. That's how he saw me. As a woman who needed to calm down and become an amoeba. A woman who needed to be in a place full of sheets and white walls; pills, capsules, tablets under her tongue. I'd get to know my roommate, drink juice with the other poor sods, attend craft workshops, read illustrated hardback books. Until one day the patients blow up balloons and draw going-away posters with coloured crayons because I've been discharged and allowed to return to society. I held in a need to heave that was a thousand times stronger than a cramp; a contraction a thousand times worse than an open sore, appendicitis, the evil eye. I became a toad and in one go, like a poisonous stream of piss, I threw up our ten years as a couple all over the table, the chair and the sofa. And faced with the damage, he didn't know whether to mop up, hug me or call an ambulance and finally have me committed. The child looked at us from between the table legs and understood it all like an adult. Inside, everything was splinters. The little one staring at me with a homemade blade in his mouth. I got up shakily: I had lost my home. I went out into the fields. I'd be less lost if I heard someone on the radio say that war had broken out. Nature was laughing at me; this old veteran was no longer the mistress around here. Insects crawled up onto my body. I stayed there, looking at the sky, rolling around in the weeds, and when it was over I went inside. My boys were watching a game show on television and eating hamburgers. The smell of fried food was in the air. Let's get married, I said. And one minute later, without taking his eyes off the TV, my man said: Sure.

Today champagne is being drunk by the glass. I have high heels on my feet for the first time. A waist I didn't know I had. My hair shines. Outside, two squirrels are swaggering around. We're all inebriated. Even the rocks. And there is a long table, the rouge stains set off against the white linen. Someone leads me to the centre of the dance floor and spins me around, teaches me the one, two, three, makes me laugh. My laughter doesn't seem believable to me. I touch my smile with my fingers. And the guests dance wildly and the women rotate their swan necks three hundred and sixty degrees, and some of them fall down the slope into the woods and are never seen again. More guests have disappeared than remain. The neighbours are asleep or dead in their rickety beds. The air is dense and every so often it shimmers. My husband comes and goes, gives me tongueless kisses, strokes my shoulder. Even the animals look at him with respect. But before the dances of death, in a makeshift chapel, a parish priest who's even less religious than I am says in an affected voice: 'We are gathered here today in the presence of God and these witnesses to celebrate before the Almighty and in the name of our holy religion, the marriage between this man and this woman.' This woman being me. 'Do you take this woman, whose hand you hold, to be your lawfully wedded wife? Do you solemnly promise, before God and these witnesses, that you will love, honour and cherish her; and that, forsaking all others for her alone, you will faithfully perform to her all the duties which a husband owes to a wife, while God grants you life?' I do. But I couldn't hear a thing. Just babbling, buzzing. Everyone's watching me, I'm the main attraction. 'Do you take this man, whose hand you hold, to be your lawfully wedded husband? Do you solemnly promise, before God and these witnesses, that you will love, honour and cherish him; and that, forsaking all others for him alone, you will faithfully perform to him all the duties which a wife owes to a husband, while God grants you life?' While God grants me life, and my legs run down the road towards a parallel life. And in my mind I still have the strength and the will to sink a knife into the flesh of a cow. And before my 'I do', I see myself covered in a coating of grass. 'Let this be the seal of your mutual faith and your mutual affection and happiness, a remembrance of this sacred service, and of the sacrosanct bonds of marriage, by which you are bound in holy matrimony till death do you part.' But how will it part us? Which of us will see the other's corpse? Who will bury whom? 'Forasmuch as this man and woman have consented together in holy wedlock, and have witnessed the same before God and this company, and have declared the same by joining hands, I pronounce that they are husband and wife. Those whom God has joined together let not man put asunder.' And everyone whooped like jackals, like hyenas, and I searched desperately for my stag. I searched for my little son too, but he was hiding. And there was no one, no one and nothing that could stop me. And they lifted us up in chairs, twirled us around in their arms and 'Hurrah!' 'Long live the newly-weds!' 'Hallelujah!' Then they threw rice at us and it got lodged in the pores of my head. I was kissed by a sequence of lumpy lips and a pack of hunting dogs with reptile tails span around in a whirlpool, upsetting the tablecloth and smashing the glasses, bottles and flowers. There are dogs running around in circles in my mind as well, or are they foals? I saw people in the open fields exchanging whispers and looking at me in astonishment. I was the empress, the bearded lady, Madame Zingare. I put a hand to my lips and instead of feeling a smile, I felt something murky, tepid and viscous dribbling from the corners of my mouth.

I was nothing but a white dress with ruffles, fitted at the waist and completely soaked in that room with a ceiling fan. My hand went wandering between my legs, but that wasn't what I needed. I scrubbed away down there for a bit, but nothing. And I squeezed myself, hit my hand until it became the hand of the other. I ripped off my garters with my teeth, pulled out the stitching with my nails, put a hand on my heart, wet the nape of my neck and splashed myself with perfume, undressing over and over. I changed my knickers. I tried to smell myself but no luck, even though I stretched my neck almost to the point of breaking it. I wanted to sleep face down. Face sideways. Face up. I grabbed the scissors with a swipe of my hand, cut off my fringe and left it on the pillow. Now there are two of us. The fan was rotating more and more slowly, advancing upon me threateningly. The phone was silent. The mattress a puddle. The jute curtains rustling slowly. He'd promised to arrive early for our night of passion. Drop the child off at the widow's place and come straight over. It's not my fault they leave me here, vulnerable, with my guts hanging out. I didn't know how long I'd been waiting for him, but after opening and closing my legs so many times, they were beginning to go numb. I jumped up. It hurt not having a bra on. Then I paced around on the bed, got down on all fours. I laughed, wrapped up in tulle, as I saw myself in the tacky, peeling mirror. A Hollywood actress, that's what I was, charming and tragic. I got in the bath and splashed about a bit. But I still didn't have what I needed, nothing was calming me down. He's still not here and I do a somersault, tie myself up, untie myself. If he doesn't come, I'll begin on my own, the appetiser, the pre-drinks. The warm-up. There's a smell of raw meat in the hotel and I inhale it. The wet dress is weighing me down. I struggle to free myself from the tangle of seaweed, from the fabric of the slip that's gripping my throat. I wet a finger with saliva knowing it won't be enough, that it'll never have the brute force I need. I'm indifferent, too naked in my body. I want to be punched, to be shaken hard. I want something thrusting at me. I call the concierge and wake him up, he talks like his eyes are glued shut. I order a martini and specify that I'd like it without olives but with two ice cubes and a slice of lemon. He turns on music for love-making, his voice sounds sympathetic. A bride in waiting. If only they could see her now. He offers to bring me a soft drink, tries to cheer me up. I hang up. My high-voltage striptease begins. On top of the toilet. I sway, shimmy, grind. I stick out my tongue. Strut around the room in my heels. I'm my own horny audience in the medicine cabinet's reflection. When it ends, I flush the toilet. The groom still hasn't arrived. This must all be the child's doing.

Indifferent, I sat in the back of the car in my yellow shorts, suitcase in hand, moving my eyebrows up and down, trying out my crazy face in the interests of practice. Acting normal, then suddenly freezing for no apparent reason and staring straight ahead. Learning how to look someone in the eye with undivided attention, but at the same time make it obvious that I'm not really there. The look I'm going for is Zelda Fitzgerald en route to Switzerland, and not for the chocolate or watches, either. With my knees under my chin, I devour the road as it stretches sinuously ahead. I bite on the window. My husband gestures at me to stop in the rearview mirror. His gesture says, We discussed this yesterday and agreed it was for the best. For all three of us. My cure is approaching, I can see it coming. A thick mirror separates us, me and her, me and the woman I'll be when I get out. I burst into laughter and my son turns around and looks at me curiously. Yes, it's your mother laughing. They're such imbeciles. Father and son, in unison. Birthed by the same woman. I'm broken, my stitches are undone. I'm wearing shoes with no laces and my shorts keep falling down. In my suitcase there's a little notepad with coloured pages, but what could I write down beyond images that don't mean anything? The road is empty and the weather report is announcing clear skies all weekend. You'll be able to relax in the sunshine, my husband says. The car has no trouble with the hills. He had it checked by the mechanic to make sure it was up to the trip. I should have snuck out at night and punctured the tyres with a needle. We have enough petrol to get to Siberia, there and back through the dirty snow piled up on the roadside. This is how the novel begins. The character sitting in the back is being taken somewhere far away. She looks meek, like a schoolgirl almost, with her shorts and her ponytail. But actually, she can scare away dogs and has bullet-wounds for eyes. She can actually see the trees sent spinning by the moving car. They overlap and intertwine, merging into one. They're not trees but a feeling of elation. A nauseous, guilty mouth. In the sky, underground and everywhere in between. Something's missing. The looks from my men are like kicks in the ribs. The two of them are singing softly in English, *love me, love me, say that you love me*, and I block them out with Mozart, Divertimento in D major, K334. We're here! he says. So this pile of uneven stones with a chimney on top is going to be my new home. For breakfast, I'll be having toast with plum jam made by a band of disturbed inpatients. Just like me. I'll work in the vegetable garden, take part in the craft workshops and sleep on a narrow mattress. The patients in the beds next to mine will have nightmares. Just like me. I'll walk around among half-smoked cigarettes. In the prime of life and in freefall. I'll wake the dead, that's how I'll keep my mind busy. I'll get them to jump over the fence like little sheep. Goodbye to morbid sexual anxiety. The three of us get out of the car looking like overwhelmed tourists. A photo here, a photo there. I think that now we'll have a tour of the facilities, the swimming pool, the games room, the dining hall. I think, now I'm on my honeymoon, like the other women. But instead someone grabs hold of my arms and squeezes them energetically. Welcome, they say, pushing me slightly. And I see how easily my husband and my son, who were at my side not a second ago, wave goodbye, saying see you later, beautiful, see you later, Mummy. Everything happens so quickly after that. I hear the engine and they're already rolling away through the hills, already singing another song. I turn around. I see a hallway full of closed doors. Someone forces me forwards. They shut me away.

On the first morning of all the other mornings, I was lying with my fingers hanging off the edge of the bed. A doctor came over. His crooked eyeglasses above me, his four pupils. I dreamt I'd left my baby asleep under acid rain. I dreamt I hadn't been able to bring him with me and he was looking at me from a long way away. I'm sorry. What's that you were saying? What was I saying? You were saying sorry. No, it was just a dream. Do I have to get up? You don't have to do anything. So I can stay in bed? Do people here go about their business during the day? You can do as you please. My husband paid for me to do as I please? You're free to leave whenever you like. Isn't this the new world? It's just somewhere that's a bit calmer than other places. And off he went, dragging his feet like all tormented doctors do. I lay there watching a small iridescent fly hit the glass of the window again and again until it collapsed, scattering pieces of its bright blue wings over my bed. I didn't see anyone else breathing nearby. No one was spying on me. Except for me. Getting up, I felt happy to be in the care of an establishment that wasn't unlike a hotel and seemed perfectly clean and comfortable. I went down to the dining hall feeling alive. I was alone. Someone had come back to life. I said hello to everyone and even asked their names. Normally, I don't care what people are called, what difference does it make. I kissed some cheeks, shook some hands and gave some encouraging pats on the back. They all seemed to be saying things like God help you or blessed art thou. The nurses and other health staff covered me in saliva. Mwah. Mwah. Someone was yelling that they wanted Rohypnol. Interesting. I crossed the dining hall with its smell of instant soup and went out into the grounds. There's a high wall separating us from a villa and its pack of German shepherds. The pornographic lyrics of a *cumbia* song float towards me from somewhere. One man's reading a newspaper. A president's been in a plane crash. Another man says something about a father killing his daughter in the middle of the Christmas holidays. Only now, as I play with my hair, do I realise that I haven't seen any women around; that is, with the exception of two females I wouldn't exactly consider to belong to the category. My husband has shut me away with men. Shaved heads are all I can see; they look like walnuts. I smell of testosterone. One man coughs and another clears his throat. They're all smokers. Nothing but deep, leaden voices. And if the doctors and patients conspire to keep me in bed? A man dressed in white winks at me. Why did my husband bring me here? To see how long I can hold out. To sicken the nymphomaniac. I drink my angel-hair soup at a round table and when I finish the plates are replaced with a game of cards which appears to keep us all entertained. A teammate pretends to be signalling for a card and looks at me with eyes that telegraph cock. At night, I hear barking come over the wall like something that belongs to another life. I slip away through the sheets. How many of the people who've slept here are now dead. Then he appears. His jawbone in my mouth. His eyes on my arse. I want to make him disappear, go up in flames, but I can't. I let the balsam of desire carry me away. And I don't even think about my son.

Until you tell me what happened I'm going to keep running away. I won't want to touch you. I'll be in a state of alert. I wish he'd keep his voice down. Shut up, they don't know me here yet. Painful silence. The therapist lets us suffer. Your husband says he's in a permanent state of alert, what do you make of that? Neither of us knows what to do with our body next to the other person's, our arms hanging down, sexless, like friends. In theory they've provided us with this therapeutic interval, and the babysitter singing lullabies in the room next door, so we can resolve our marital problems. So you can try to open your wounds, says the professional, and I laugh and then say, I'm sorry. Surely all that singing must be boring the baby to death. Here I am in this ridiculous office overlooking the grounds and their artificial grass, with cups of tea on a tray in front of me and relaxing music in the background. Music to help you think, says the professional. Music to make you want to bang your head against the wall. My husband's face is deep red. He's a bull charging at me. My husband's dick is a thousand times bigger than the other man's but he doesn't know how to use it. Or his tongue. I listen to the list of suggestions the professional has for us, but still fervently believe we'll get divorced because he doesn't know how to use his tongue. It's a reptile's tongue. The tiny tongue of a sleeping snake. Never a long lick, a love bite, a lap. A docile tongue that doesn't know how to strangle you. I'm not sure what I make of the presence of a third person. I don't know what they expect me to say. I look at him and I can see he's an unhappy husband, but I need to piss and you can go fuck yourself, I've been horny since I met you, horny and neurotic and cursed. What's wrong with you? says my husband. Do you have some sort of symbiosis? It's *neurosis*, I say. And what does your neurosis have to do with anything? Everybody's got some kind of neurosis. You gave me a strange look. What are you thinking about? An image crossed my mind. I'm sorry, I say. It's the image of a jet-black horse with bulging eyes, eyes out of their sockets. The horse crushes me and I writhe beneath it. I'm sorry, I say again. You never act like a normal person, you're never relaxed, he says. He's on the attack. He's about to use the word cool but stops himself just in time. I don't know what I say to him. It's that you don't fuck me. Well, when you're like this I don't feel like it, I avoid you. I mean, you spend all day sulking. The therapist says the words tolerance and mutual respect, and we hear him as though we were underwater. These servile republicans… toler what? He asks again about my husband's state of alert. I refuse to answer. They want to make me sing like a bird. I try to control my perspiration, my heart rate, I don't want anything to give me away. Why do you think he feels he's in danger? A trick question if ever there was one. What do you think is causing this state? I know exactly what's causing this state and I could tell you all about it with my eyes closed. The whole thing bores me. The shadow cast by another man won't do. I'm bored of this, I say, and begin to nod off. The baby, who's no longer really a baby, starts crying next door. The babysitter has no clue how to comfort him. She should have chosen something else to do with her life. I'm going to club you to death, I said. How could I have reached the point of saying to him, I'm going to club you to death? Call the police, don't be scared. No, actually don't call them. Sue me for negligence, like you see in those Hollywood films with mothers who've lost it but don't end up killing themselves, and instead return to their family and bake chocolate brownies on Sundays. You *are* negligent, he says. I wanted much more for myself. Should we try family therapy and have the baby take part? I bullshit him. You're juvenile, he says, under the therapist's look of contained approval. They like each other. You're a shitty husband, I thought, and hugged him tight. I ignored the professional, who was noting down something cryptic and probably very interesting, and went over to squeeze my man, I squeezed him so hard I wrung out his guts. I groped at him hoping he wouldn't reject me, wouldn't toss me aside. And he didn't. My saviour.

He left and I stayed behind looking at the grounds as though they were a cliff. He left and he took his baby with him. I felt like I'd ruined everything. A breath of irrationality had set fire to my existence and I found myself trying to keep up appearances with a loaded gun on my hands. I wanted to pull the trigger so badly. Unbelievable how much noise those damned birds make. Outside, nature was following its sunset ritual. Some people left the dining hall with a tangerine or a bunch of grapes and a pair of binoculars to watch the birds migrate from the continent. Apparently they find the repetitive flapping of wings moving. They smiled at me on their way outside, but then they realised what was going on and quickened their step. I felt voluptuous as I strode down the hallway, my tits above my shirt collar, slant-eyed, my hair straightened, a victorious smile on my face and the gun raised up high. The professional was close behind me. I saw him in the glass doors and his shoes stuck to me like chewing gum. He was still worried about the way I behaved during the counselling session with my husband. He ran a few steps to catch up and then, flustered, asked me to follow him into his office. Please, come this way. But when he saw my hand in the shape of a revolver, my index finger miming the action of pulling the trigger, he stepped back. What a wuss. Once he'd caught his breath he urged me to enter his office and locked the door behind me. I will allow myself to say the following, knowing it's an intrusion into your private life, he began, still panting a little, and I yawned. He was tempted to ask me to chop off my hand, but he knew it would be illegal. I hate having to waste my time with people who repeat platitudes, myself included. I see that behind the beige curtain a group of inpatients are chasing ducks around. He says my husband feels powerless against the figure of the unknown man, who's like a bulldozer. That the air in my house is turning foul. That he said he'd prefer me to stay another week. All of this was discussed behind my back. It's official, I've been grounded. I want the day to end once and for all. I want night to begin, for them to let me out so that I can face the animals. In the end I said I felt responsible, that I was going to rethink my role as a wife and as a mother, that it would be helpful to stay another week, and I allowed my hand to return to its five-fingered shape. He tried to get me to confess, but as soon as he saw the look on my face he opened the door. I went out into the hallway and ran to my bedroom. The steam from the showers blinded me. I called my husband. You have reached the X family. Please leave a message after the beep and we'll call you back as soon as we can. Thank you. It's always the same. How do they manage to keep going, how are they so similar. Even a herd of goats can be told apart by the way each animal lifts its chin. I ran through the hallway, took a shortcut outside and leapt over the danger signs warning about the demolition in progress. I walked and didn't see anyone. What might the father and son be up to. I imagine them naked in the pool under a stream of nice warm water, checking out each other's peckers. I see them playing with the hose, drawing letters in the air. They're squatting in the garden pulling up vegetables and munching on the leafy greens. Afterwards, they'll enjoy a dessert of ice cream under the moon and the father will tell the son the name of each star. The son pointing. The father pushing the son on the swing, the son pushing the father. I see them gradually forgetting me tonight. I see them forgetting me tomorrow night as well.

The two of them were on the opposite side of the road with their bags and packed lunches. Apparently it's better to keep children away from places like this. I went down for breakfast at dawn and found myself in an empty dining hall for the first time. Then I walked outside with wet hair and my swimsuit pressing against my tits and smiled at the two of them. Big day, he said, and we got into the four-wheel drive he'd borrowed from a concerned uncle. For several miles, and until we'd passed the toll booths, we were happy, our faces to the wind, singing along to an eighties classic on the radio and squeezing each other's shoulders from time to time. Life flows along. For several miles south we were a typical family, mother-father-son with their SPF25 sunscreen, and a thermos and jackets for when the sun goes down. We made it through the police checkpoints and passed a tree nursery filled with tall pines and eucalyptus. Then the road began to smell of salt and we parked and my husband got our little boy ready for his first trip to the sea. I watched myself in the rearview mirror and didn't see anything out of the ordinary. My boyfriend (I liked calling him that on occasion) was telling me something, I've no idea what, some story from when he was little. I felt like a good wife listening to him, saying attentively, aha, aha. We opened the boot and took out the polka-dot beach umbrella, the carefully packed lunches and the thermos. He'd taken care of everything. The baby pointed excitedly towards the sea. A good sign. Don't forget to film the exact moment he goes in, said my husband, as excited as my son about the advancing, retreating hurricane of blue. We were in the tropics. The three of us jumping around in the sand, getting sunburnt and laughing. I saw an elderly woman in a swimming costume and a thick layer of sunscreen beaming at us from her tent, happy to see a family together. Everything was going well. The coastguard's flag showed the sea was calm and it was safe to swim. Lying on the sand were the unused flags: medium hazard, high hazard, danger (no swimming), missing child. Some people were snoozing in makeshift hammocks hung with coloured rope, and others were sunbathing naked. One of them caught my attention, he was so red that his features had become diluted behind his burgundy skin. There were lots of toddlers running around in circles, stealing people's shoes and making little whirlpools in the sand. Mine threw himself in with the clan and in no time they became a pack of wild babies. My husband asked me to put sunscreen on his buttocks and then lay down. A second later, he was out cold. I didn't want to meet the eye of any of the women with books open who were looking to each side in the hope of a distraction. I didn't want to be under anyone's watch. So I stretched out alongside him and proceeded to get burned to the sound of the shouting babies running rampant in the background. I might have dozed off for a few seconds, who knows, but the point is that when I turned over on the uncomfortable plastic sun lounger I noticed that my husband, who was fast asleep, had an erection the likes of which I'd never seen on him before. I lay there looking at him, stunned, but his face gave nothing away; I couldn't tell where the erection was coming from. And this bothered me because I knew it must have been coming from somewhere, this desire that had clearly not been brought on by me, flopping as I was like a crème brûlée by his side. And I believe it was then, if my memory serves me right, that it all began. I shook him a little – he says it was a lot – and pulled his trunks to one side. The woman in the swimming costume told me off, reminding me there were children present, that it was a family beach, and that there were places for that sort of behaviour. My husband was still dead to the world but that thing was so alive it started to cloud my vision and I felt sure he was hiding something from me. I was jealous of his dream and wanted to see more, draw back the curtain. So I shouted: Wake up right now! Tell me exactly what's going on! And that's when he looked at me and said, You're crazy, and I punched him in the chest, and the cloud of children covered in sand froze. And then, because children always exaggerate, they began to bawl. Since we weren't their parents and since kids are hypersensitive their mothers came rushing over as though their babies were witnessing a violent sex scene and wrapped them up in garish beach towels to cover their eyes and ears. Meanwhile, a group of people taking the whole thing very seriously informed the lifeguard on duty, who took it upon himself to intervene, having found a way to be useful for a moment. My husband had just woken up. He didn't defend me at all. He threw me to the lions, to the insults, to the string of obscenities that always come out of preachers' mouths, and carried away the little boy, who had black sand on his nose and was spitting out pebbles. He left me with all those eyes on me. He didn't take any responsibility, he was a total coward. By this point, my husband wasn't hard any more, in fact he didn't even look like a man. It wasn't until we were driving over the white lines of the road in complete silence that we realised we hadn't even taken our son into the sea.

I had to relive it. It's all that's left, it's my escape, and besides, if there's one thing I've got plenty of in here it's time. I go over that night, when I went back and forth to the window, first with a lighter, then with a seven-branched candelabrum, coming and going, following his shadow. I turned the lamps on and off, over and over, to see if he was still there, if he was the type who'd weather a storm. My husband was asleep in bed with his mobile on his chest, not the least concerned about radiation. My baby was practically asleep on his feet but he still went on stumbling through the house, holding onto the curtains and the century-old coffee tables and throwing whatever he found to the floor. Ashtrays, cutlery. Maybe he was staying awake to make sure I didn't spend the night in another man's arms. It was a long time before I was finally able to put him in the cot, stop his crying, turn the pages of one of his books about astronauts or sea captains and convince him that the best thing you can do at night is sleep. Mummy's telling lies. When I moved towards the door, my husband appeared in his chequered underwear, hunting for a cigarette. He looked sweet. All men are sweet when they're half-asleep, as if something has relaxed in the triangle between their eyes, nose and mouth, something that makes them seem less like men. Where are you going? Nowhere, outside, I said. Giving two answers at once is never very effective. You're going outside? To do what? To do nothing, to take out the rubbish, I say. I need to come up with something more creative next time. Leave the bag over by the door, I'll take it out tomorrow. He fucks

everything up when he acts like a good husband. I'll have
to grit my teeth and stick a pillow between my legs. Or
escape as soon as he falls asleep, jump the fence. He puts
the kettle on, adds wood to the fire and starts clicking his
fingers. He doesn't seem about to go anywhere. I waited
for the water to boil, not knowing where the other man
was. I could no longer hear the ting ting ting of the ring
on his finger against the fence. I could no longer feel the
death rattle behind the windows. My husband looked at
me, his eyes narrowed to slits, as he snacked on our little
boy's biscuits. He was acting like everything was perfectly
normal whilst standing in my way, blocking my path. I did
all kinds of things, like checking the baby hadn't strangled
himself on the string of his toy bunny on wheels, clearing
the table, wiping down the kitchen counter. I sat in the open
window and took a few drags of the Gauloise covered in
marks from his lips. Another woman's son was sleeping in
the house. Why bother giving birth, I repeated in my head,
looking at the tangle of weeds beginning to take on the
colours of dawn. He was sitting by the fire with his chin
in his hands, playing chess alone. After moving one of the
pawns, he seemed to be on the verge of saying something
like let's expand our family, or let's make a little brother for
him to play with. But he moved a piece on the chessboard
instead, and then said he was done for the night. He wanted
to know how late I was going to hang around down here, to
which I said, I'm coming, I'll be there soon, you go ahead.
He gave me a peck on the lips but he seemed to be getting
further and further away. It was like we were two statues.
And just as I was about to leave, he called to me from the
bathroom. He told me to be careful. Of what, I said, without
going towards him, without letting him see me. You know
what I'm talking about. Just be careful, that's all. And he
went straight to sleep. As soon I stepped outside, I saw him

and forgot about everything that had come before, about the smouldering house, about my little soldier sleeping with his eyes open like a rabbit, about all those days of anguished anticipation. And I devoured him. Because that, my dear son, is what the night is for.

Life does not flow, I thought as they were sentencing me to a series of consultations with various professionals as a result of that ill-fated trip to the sea. One of the exercises I had to do involved shutting myself in a room with a mirror and looking at my reflection for hours. The idea was that when it was over I'd be able to tell them what I'd seen. But you're all wasting your energy. I don't need to look at my reflection to know I'm a piece of shit. What's the point. Why didn't I keep my mouth shut. Forget I said anything. Why do you say you're a piece of shit? Is this what you think of yourself, or what you think other people think of you? I almost don't bother answering at this point. I already know I'm a piece of shit. There was a strong smell of roast chicken coming from outside. Later, they'd watch a movie on human relations and follow it with a discussion. They asked: Do you miss your loved ones? And my head was in a tank of water and I saw my son with the face of a little child, dirty cheeks, red bottom, blonde hair. Do you miss your country? they went on. A Polish country bumpkin. A strawberry-blonde. An exile just like me. And they continued making noise with their desiccated words. They were practically talking over one another, and in my mind: Glenn Gould playing English Suite No. 1. Why didn't you make it into the sea? they kept asking. It's symbolic, wouldn't you say? Why couldn't you bring yourselves to take the final step? And I saw myself in my little swimsuit, my two pink dots in the wind, my sandy vagina, my haggard three-year-old eyes. I bet it's got something to do with that, I thought, but didn't give them anything. If they want to analyse me, they can do it without clues. I'm three years old. I ran away from my family when mummy duck and daddy duck weren't paying attention. Their argument's escalating and I wander off, getting lost in the water along the shore that looks like saliva. All of a sudden I don't recognise anyone around me. It's all colourful swimsuits and moving mouths but no one knows who I am. I spend the whole afternoon alone, going from tent to tent, eating what I find, leftover pastries, letting my head be petted by men reading the paper with their feet sunk into the sand, knocking down sandcastles, crawling along the sea wall. Until a large man asked me where my parents were and what my name was. Back then it didn't occur to me to lie. He grabbed me and lifted me onto his shoulders, and the whole beach began clapping their hands to help the missing child find her parents. I'm a little monkey being carried on the shoulders of a lifeguard while all around us I hear clap, clap, clap. What do they want? The tattooed lifeguard pats my knee reassuringly as I ride tall on his shoulders. His hand is very big. I'm still a little girl but I like the feel of the nape of his neck rubbing against my swimsuit while people run around me. They continue clapping and I throw my head back and as we gallop and I see only sky-blue. I'm a Russian circus star and everyone's cheering for me. I'm an acclaimed child performer. The lifeguard's already hoisted the missing-child flag. They should also have one for children who've run away. And at the end of the pier I see two figures racing towards us so fast they almost trip. I see two elephants stretching out their trunks to inhale me. It's them. With my legs I cling to my saviour's neck, but the female elephant sucks me up and gives me a hug. Everyone celebrates the reunion. On the loudspeaker they thank the public for their solidarity, and there's a murmur of approval. I'm tempted to say, Wait, keep looking, this isn't my family! But as usual, the thought occurs to me too late. The professionals look at me. What are you thinking? Has something occurred to you? Now I see that my baby wanted to sit down with some strangers on their beach mat, keep nice and quiet, and when they packed up to leave, go with them, following the train of their lives. Let's wrap this session up, they said in unison, and I kept my mouth shut. I left feeling hungover, stumbling, barely holding myself up by the wall of the corridor. The two chatterboxes had been kicking me in the head. Who am I? I spat out and laughed. Who? I said to myself again, laughing louder. I was that mother who climaxes in front of her son, that baby daughter who catches a glimpse of her father. A few of the inpatients said, Shhh, let us sleep in peace! I staggered outside as best I could and walked around until I reached the middle of the grounds, then I lay down on the grass. The landscape surrounding me was jet black. Something was floating in the air, a feeling of dawn, of childhood, of the morning when I was still half-asleep and they dressed me for a train journey, putting my shoes on opposite sides to correct my club feet. That night, the sky was identical to the one I saw from the shoulders of a giant when I was lost and nowhere to be found.

When I woke up, I was inside my woods. Like someone who discovers they're missing an arm or an eye, I noticed I no longer felt any love for my son. I left the humid bedroom looking for clarity, but outside it was raining. I heard the quiet cries of animals and the feeling of being in a wood intensified. I thought that seeing the stag, having the stag stare right at me, might help, so I went to look for him. But instead of his antlers, I found nurses. I walked through the building feeling nothing. I walked and walked, bumping into a door and a staircase. When I got somewhere, they sat me down and blindfolded me. I don't know why I was sitting down or why I'd been blindfolded, but what did it matter if I was still burning and I couldn't feel that love. Someone span me around counting one, two, three! and then they let me go, leaving something like a needle in my hand. People were touching me. I didn't know whether to fight them off or accept that everything, even my aversion to my baby, was a dream. The exultant cheering guided me, cold, cold, warmer, hot, hot, burning! And apparently my needle found the piñata because something exploded and they all clapped. I stayed blindfolded, they told me I could look now but I wanted that pleasant darkness to continue. Eventually, the other people grew impatient and removed the blindfold themselves. Streamers, colourful signs, gifts, and me covered in confetti. We wish you all the very best for your new life. They gave me cards and good-luck charms and led me away. I was leaving. It was the end. Yet for me it was the beginning because out there is where gloom and pessimism lie. They opened the main door. There they were. The father all dressed up, the son wearing his football kit, the two of them holding hands. My bitter sweetheart, my little leapfrog. Welcome to us. They let me move towards them while everything behind me faded away. My husband and my son. The three of us hugged. The baby was already walking, had more teeth, more hair and an expanded vocabulary that included coing coing and taca taca. My husband told a joke to lighten the mood: Now you're finally out we'll be able to live in peace. And they greeted me as if to say I was ready, I'd graduated, it was time to get on with my life. He stopped the car at the side of the road, and on the banks of a river I hadn't seen before he told me to shut my eyes. Once again, I stopped seeing. Our little boy couldn't contain his happiness, he was frantic with excitement. My husband pressed a button and the roof opened up like a peacock's feathers. I stayed put and they got out to see how it looked. Back on the road, giddy with joy, my son raised his hands and let the air rush between his fingers. He threw stones into the river. I told him to stop, that it was dangerous, that the wind could carry him away, but he didn't listen to me. I complained to my husband, who did nothing. That's how we drove the miles that separated my house in the countryside from that other place, which had already fallen into the apathy of things past. They asked me how I was, if I'd made friends, if I'd brought them any presents. My head was already flying backwards but my husband accelerated to make the journey even more exciting. When we drove into our town, we were escorted through the streets as though to the altar. There it all was, existing once again: the tractors, the sheds, the neighbours smoking in their doorways. I walked into my house and everything shone. There had been changes: a microwave with the time flashing, a table-cloth embroidered with the petals of large flowers, a new

117

cordless phone with a notepad next to it. I sat down on the sofa facing the fireplace. Their movements were halos of light. The reflection of the first knife I ever dreamt of was in my hand again. If instead of being punished I'd been admitted on medical grounds, if instead of a place to rest it had been a real mental asylum, I wouldn't have this dagger in my hand. Scared, I moved towards the glass door I'd once crashed through, which now had a mosquito mesh on it. I opened the door and ran outside to look for him. I needed to see the tips of his antlers. Oh, stag of mine, darling stag, my one and only. I hope you're out there.

The decorations looked great, I could be proud of myself there. Banners with little bumper cars on them, the table set with mini plates of finger food, a party bag for each guest and the birthday boy all dressed up. Bright colours, music, everything a party's supposed to have. My little lamb is already two years old and in my mind I'm still pushing, because he's coming, he's almost there, you can see his tiny head now. When it was time to blow out the candles, my husband stood behind me and lots of cameras aimed at us. There we were for all eternity in the photo, decorated and walled in. Then my little boy, because he's not a baby any more they said, spat out his chocolate banana cake and ran away. I chased him, rugby-tackled him, kissed him, breathed him in, and then he escaped again. The neighbours' children played hide-and-seek, tag, and duck, duck, goose, because games here are the same as they've always been. I poured myself the dregs of yesterday's wine, swirled them around and walked through the birthday party like any host would, my chest anointed. The other mothers showed their approval, tiny threads of banana hanging from their teeth. Everything was turning out wonderfully. I finished my glass in the swing and poured myself the dregs, just the dregs, of another bottle, and then another, and I drank to myself, and to the birthday party I'd managed to organise. And I don't know why, but at that point my gaze fell on a mound of earth in the garden. At first, I didn't understand. I kept looking at it the way you might images of events that took place millions of years ago, the past looked at from the present. Then I felt the dog leap up onto my lap and sink a tooth into me. Of course. Poor Bloody was down there. That's where my husband and I had put the dog, but only at noon, by which time its eyes were full of flies. It had been there the whole night with a bullet in it, unburied. Entrails all over the place. So dead that it didn't even let out a last howl. And as I was looking at its remains, I heard the gun go off. The kids were skipping over the makeshift grave, singing and laughing and holding hands. And I don't know if it was that, or the rancid wine, or the mouths smeared with banana, but something made me rush inside and shut myself in my bedroom, slamming the door behind me. I hope you all die, every last one of you. As usual, he came knocking on my door. Darling, honey, sugar, sweetheart, my bunny rabbit, my love, I can't remember all the names he called me. And I said nothing. Are you okay? And I still said nothing. Come out, all the guests are leaving, don't ruin this. Where are the party bags? And I said, Why don't you leave me the hell alone and die. Just die, my love. I thought I could hear the dog barking and snarling on the other side of the door, protesting at my having killed him. I pushed the door open and went out, striding straight through the dining room where the goodbye fondling was already underway, the searching for lost coats, the children crying because they didn't want to leave, and I got into the convertible and accelerated. I don't know if I put it in first or third gear. Where are you going? Are you crazy? You don't have your license, I heard him say from the house. As I drove off, I shouted: He's all yours, he's my present to you. I'll hand him over gift-wrapped, you deserve him more than I do. I'll give him to you. Our son. By that point, people had come outside to see what was going on and were whispering to each other that I'd lost it again. Then more gates, more sheep, more chickens squashed on the tarmac, more abandoned windmills, more boats sunk in lakes, more chimneys spewing out black, more animal pens, and then I stopped. I jumped out and went inside. His princess was in the window, but there was no one else around. Neither him nor his wife. No trace of either of them. Had they abandoned their special daughter? I looked in every room, looked at the bed they fuck in, looked at their bathroom, at his toothbrush, at everything he looks at from the minute he gets up, and then I collapsed into the embroidered armchair in the living room. Upstairs, the daughter moans. Downstairs, the tick-tock of a grandfather clock. I fell asleep and dreamt of the sweet and hollow sound of an antler, of him on his back, his hair stuck to my skin, until I heard giggles. There they were, coming down the path, their baskets overflowing with mushrooms. Was I ancient history? I went outside to wait for them. The woman looked at me with horror. He gestured for her to go upstairs to their little girl and then took me by the arm. We walked fifty yards away, maybe more. We were face-to-face but we didn't say a thing. Speaking is so disgusting, after all. We kissed. I saw his face change, maybe he was looking at the marks left by the glass. My tongue on his tongue was a painkiller and I knew that was the reason, that was why he was kissing me. And it was so powerful, that kiss, that taste of salty blood, that stopping of death in its tracks. Then my husband arrived on a motorcycle that was too small for him and made him look like he was fourteen. My two bulls, my stallions, my pawns, suddenly together. No words were needed. My men understood each other with gestures alone and off they went together into the open fields, stopping where I couldn't hear them. I saw the shadow cast by their bodies, the profiles of the two of them facing each other. Mother and daughter appeared at the window, one paler than the other. I watched them squaring up for the duel, but then the tension dissipated and it was like two long-lost brothers catching up, reminiscing about their childhood in the family home, discussing how to settle their dead parents' debts. The sun began to set over their heads, the gentle light of dusk slowly tinting their bodies. A soft, steady rain fell on them. And as they talked, my life came and went. I don't know what was being said, only that they weren't raising their voices any more. Something about the way they stepped a little to the side, the way they nodded their heads slightly told me they'd understood each other. One of them yawned. The other laughed. They had reached an agreement. The Siamese twins parted and one of them came towards me. I was trembling. Who would it be? Who would be my black-market buyer? What would become of my life, in which home would I live, what would they call me, whoever had chosen me? He coughed and I knew it was my husband, the most loyal of the two. We walked towards the open-top car in silence. It was a silence more complete than all those that had come before it. As we drove home in the rain, I noticed a row of cypresses. Are those new? I asked. They've always been there, he said. He didn't stop at the front door but I could tell the party was over because a few blue balloons were drifting over the minefield that was our garden. Is the baby asleep inside? He's not a baby any more, he said. But what I understood was, he's not *your* baby any more. We drove into the woods, the wheels leaving tracks in the earth. Not many animals were awake. The stag didn't appear, but I was there instead. He turned off the engine and relaxed, letting out a breath he'd been holding in for too long. So what do you want to do? A question was the last thing I'd been expecting. I thought the outcome had been positive, or negative, and that he'd tell me how much time I had left, in weeks, in days. I thought he'd cry. I hadn't been expecting a question. What do you think? But I couldn't say a word. Poor thing. And my whole life was a shrill whistle piercing his silence. The trees in the wood were like tigers in heat. I won't be able to forget, he said, and for the first time he was serious. Another silence, this one more stifling than the last. The buzzing in my ears plummeted to the ground like a dead bird. There was nothing to say after the look he gave me. What could I possibly add. When he saw I wasn't going to put up a fight, he lit a cigarette and said, Besides, they're expecting a child. Two, actually. They're having two tiny twins. And although we tried to stay serious, we couldn't help but laugh. About what, I don't know. The sound of the words two tiny twins maybe. And what if *we* have one? Another child? The question gave him a coughing fit. And then we were in hysterics again. Another child, us! The two of us sat there laughing together for the very last time like a happily married couple. I got out without opening the door – the convertible happens to be a very practical model for break-ups – and he turned and saw me disappear into the undergrowth. At first, I felt nothing but pain. The kind of pain a person doesn't share, not even with herself. I was in mourning for a long time, but there came a moment when, like the widow who unlocks her front door for the first time, who eats dinner in silence for the first time, who gets into bed alone for the first time, I felt a sadness that was exhilarating, wild.